THE GUARDIAN PROGRAM

Book One of The Terre Hoffman Chronicles

Second Edition

Copyright © 2020, 2021 by Herman Steuernagel

This is a work of fiction. Names, characters, places, and incidents either are the product of the author's imagination or are used fictitiously. Any resemblance to actual persons, living or dead, events or locales is entirely coincidental.

All international rights reserved. No part of this publication may be reproduced, stored or transmitted in any form or by any means, electronic, mechanical, photocopying, recording, scanning, or otherwise without written permission from the publisher. It is illegal to copy this book, post it to a website, or distribute it by any other means whether digital or printed without permission in writing from the copyright owner.

ISBN: 978-199050500-0-3 (paperback)

ISBN: 978-17771777-9-9 (ebook)

Cover by MiblArt

Edited by Novel Approach Manuscript Services

https://www.hermansteuernagel.com

THE GUARDIAN PROGRAM

HERMAN STEUERNAGEL

THE TERRE HOFFMAN CHRONICLES | BOOK ONE

Chapter One

Andersen Air Force Base, Guam
May 2052

"Not again!"

Alarms blared across Andersen Air Force Base, rousing Terre Hoffman from his bed. "We've got to get these proximity alarms fixed," he grumbled. "I'm sick of being woken up in the middle of the night!"

As he had been every night for the past two weeks.

"*You're* sick of it?" His wife, Cara, rolled over, pulling a pillow over her head as he turned on the light.

Terre scrambled for his clothes across the now illuminated bedroom, digging through the pile of laundry he had collected together for the current day's wash.

"I thought that was why they brought that kid in?" Cara continued. "What's his name?"

"Kristopher, bae. And yes, that's why he's here. *Supposedly.*" Terre pulled a white t-shirt over his head before stepping into and pulling up his pair of designer slacks. Despite being required to dress professionally at the office, he'd ditch the tie and suit jacket for today. He could already feel the sweat on his back from the heat of the day. He looked at his watch again to make sure.

Only 3 a.m. and it was already a hundred degrees; he wasn't sure if the heat or the humidity bothered him more. Luckily, Terre spent most of his day in an air-conditioned technology center.

"Do you have to go in? Can't he take care of it?" Cara rolled over again, shielding her eyes against the light of the lamp. She grabbed the bedsheet and wrapped it around her body, as if cocooning herself against the glare. The white of the blanket contrasted with the dark brown skin of her back as she sat up, facing away from him.

Cara was right: Kristopher probably could take care of the situation, but there was no point in Terre staying home. He might as well be doing something if he was awake anyway. Besides, his boss required him to go in, even if it was only to monitor K's progress.

Terre grabbed a white button-down shirt from the wardrobe, pulled his arms through its sleeves, and fumbled with the buttons. His hands trembled as adrenaline raced through him. How many times had the same alarm jolted him from his sleep? He wouldn't get used to the way it clawed at his nerves.

"K's just a contractor, Cara. *I'm* the Senior IT Specialist. I've got to be there." He threw his hands in the air when she looked unconvinced. "I'm the babysitter."

He took his role as supervisor seriously, and he wasn't used to being completely useless in a situation. If he had been able to figure out how to stop the damn things to begin with, the kid would never have been brought in.

After the alarms had gone off for the third night in a row, his boss had decided it was time to call in outside help. There was little room for error when you're in charge of the network for a military base. Terre was lucky he still had a job, so he did his best not to feel emasculated by the call. And besides, although the kid wrote the software, they still didn't have an answer as to what was behind the activations, a whole two weeks after Kristopher had shown up.

"Kristopher wrote the stupid proximity detector program, and even *he* hasn't been able to figure it out."

"Why is he here, then? Can't you take care of it?" Cara sighed as she pulled the sheet off of her and grabbed a light blue t-shirt from her nightstand. She stood and pulled the shirt on over her naked torso. She was Terre's biggest fan, but she didn't understand the first thing about how these proximity detectors worked. Though, he wished he had a better understanding himself.

Terre had transferred to Guam two years earlier, hoping to provide his new family with the luxury of island life for a few years. Living on a military base took some getting used to, but it sure was hard to beat the island weather. Surf and sand were worth the sacrifices they had made to be here, but Terre knew those consolations wouldn't last forever. He hadn't planned to be away from the mainland indefinitely. Their daughter Sarah had grown up without knowing her extended family, and both he and Cara had been on edge lately. It was all adding up to a situation he no longer wanted to be in.

A smile overcame his lips as he watched Cara finish getting dressed enough to see him to the door. She insisted on seeing him out each time he left for work, even during late-night calls. She never wanted to miss saying goodbye, just in case the worst happened. Some saw it as a paranoid way of looking at life, but Terre didn't see it that way. He and Cara appreciated the simple things and never wanted to take them for granted.

After four years, it still hadn't grown old.

"It's not like I haven't tried," he replied. "But thanks for believing in me. K *wrote* the program. We'll discover the bug ten times faster with his help. Without him, I'm just shooting in the dark."

"He doesn't seem to be doing much better."

"It's not always easy to pinpoint a bug. It could be a problem with the program or with the signals. Hell, it could be a dirty sensor for all we know. There are a lot of diagnostics to run, and unless the army wants the alarm running nonstop until we find it, it's going to take time."

At this point, if the fault was nothing more than a dirty sensor, Terre would be tempted to hand in his resignation. But as was often the case, it was usually something simple that was easy to overlook. Terre tried to convince himself they were close to solving the issue, but over the last couple of days, Kristopher—or 'K,' as Terre liked to call him—had been hitting dead end after dead end. Terre couldn't see an issue with the system, and neither could K. It was all a little unsettling.

How many US Defense bases depended on these alarms for an early warning of an attack? K didn't even seem to know a specific number, and neither specialist was given any definite answers when they asked, but the number was potentially high. More was riding on the two of them than Terre wanted to know. Once they'd patched this bug, they'd push the fix to the other bases. If it was a malfunctioning sensor, he'd hang his head and submit their test results up the chain of command.

For whatever reason, the problem had first manifested itself on his base, under his watch. K couldn't access the code remotely because of its classified nature, so the military had flown him in. The contractor had needed complete access to ground zero.

"I know. It's just this entire thing makes me nervous," Cara replied. "This post was supposed to be like a vacation. You remember? That's what you told me. And even though the first year was great, this shit is getting tiring. And don't think I haven't noticed the pressure has been getting to you, too. You can be a network specialist anywhere, so why not somewhere near the beach? California has beaches, Terre! You could have worked for a tech company in Silicon Valley."

"We've gone through this, Cara. We could have, remember? But we wanted to get out and experience something new; live somewhere other than California before Sarah has to go to school. It's only a temporary placement. Once I've completed the upgrades here, we'll be back in San Francisco. Or wherever you want to go. I have unlimited options."

Cara sat back down on the edge of the bed, her head in her hands. She embedded her fingers into the curls of her hair and then rubbed her eyes as she stood, taking a deep breath.

"I know. I'm sorry. These 3 a.m. alarms are getting to me, that's all. I'm stressing out. I'm overtired. And it's affecting Sarah, too. She's falling asleep in the middle of playing." Cara sighed.

"Falling asleep while playing is what kids do." Terre attempted to smile reassuringly. "These activations are just false alarms. Nothing has come of them."

"*Yet.*" Cara looked up at him, her dark brown eyes wet. He wasn't sure if it was from being tired, or something more. She immediately looked apologetic. "I just worry," she said.

Terre nodded. He understood the sentiment, but he had signed a contract. Only a few more months and he could start entertaining other offers.

He led them out of the bedroom, down the narrow hallway that connected their small home. It was cramped, but it more than served their needs. A photograph on the wall caught his eye as he passed: Cara and himself, hands clasped in a dance during their last New Year's Eve party in San Francisco.

Cara pulled him close and ran her hand across the stubble on his chin. He would probably get an earful about the dress code for not shaving, but if he had to go in at 3 a.m., he was going to cut some corners.

"Two years is a hell of a temporary placement," she continued. "Can you promise me, once you've finished these upgrades, you'll start looking for something else? Something back on the mainland? Closer to home?"

"I promise," he relented. It might have been the sleep deprivation, but as of late, Terre had been thinking the same thing. This—living in Guam—had never been the long-term plan. He had enjoyed his time here, but it was time to build a more permanent home for his family.

Terre kissed Cara on the forehead and ran his fingers across her cheek. "We'll get this bug sorted out before you know it," he said. "I know everyone's on edge, but we're safe here."

Safe here? Who was he kidding? China and the US had been at each other's throats for the last five years, and Guam was the first line of defense. It had felt like the right thing to say, and she didn't question him, but Terre wasn't sure he fully believed it.

They made their way through the house, toward the door. He tried to suppress a yawn and failed. Cara caught it, which made them both laugh.

Terre bent over as his wife stood on her tiptoes to kiss him.

"We'll have the alarm silenced in an hour or so. Try to get some rest, and then take Sarah to the beach today. It's supposed to be a nice one."

He turned toward the door, but the sound of little feet running through the hallway made him pause. His three-year-old daughter, Sarah, stuck her head around the corner, her face scrunched up in exaggerated disgust.

"Daddy, why is the alarm going off again? I thought you said you'd fix it."

He shot his wife a *'Don't even'* glance.

"Daddy's still working on it, honey. My friend hasn't figured out what's wrong yet."

"Why can't *you* figure it out?"

"I'm trying, sweetheart. We'll have it fixed soon, okay?"

She put her hands up to her ears. "It's too loud."

"I know, but it's supposed to wake us up if we're in danger."

Her eyes went wide. "Are we in danger?"

"Not tonight, honey. It's broken. That's why we have to fix it: so it will only go off if there's something wrong."

That must have been a good enough explanation for her. Her hands still covering her ears, Sarah waddled down the hallway. Terre smiled after his daughter and wondered how, at one point not long ago, he had gotten by without her.

"I'll see you in a few hours," he said to his wife, giving her another kiss. He was just dragging his feet now; he needed to get going.

"Sounds good. Now go turn that thing off! Some of us would like to get some sleep."

"*Wait!* Dad!" Sarah came barreling back out of her room, arm outstretched, with something dangling from her wrist. "You almost fo'got your lucky charm!"

He smiled. The 'lucky charm' was a chain with a robot pendant; a trinket she had picked out for his birthday a few months ago. Cara had taken her to the store to help pick out his present. The pendant had been on display at a store off-base, and Sarah had immediately fallen in love with it.

Of course she had. Sarah: the kid that loved all things

robots. It probably had something to do with her favorite cartoon, *Milo the Robot*.

Just about everything she owned was robot themed. Even now, he smiled at her *Milo the Robot* pajamas. He hated the show, which naturally meant that Sarah loved it. And with those big brown eyes, it was impossible to say no.

At least it was educational. Terre suspected that Artificial Intelligence might be the only career path available in twenty years. Hell, IT was nearly the only career path available already. He got little time to pay attention to the news, but when he did, the stories of protests from the exponentially increasing number of people losing their jobs to automation were hard to ignore.

When Cara had given the pendant to him, he had improvised a splendid show of how much he loved the trinket. He had told her it was the perfect thing for him to wear at work; that it would be his lucky charm, and that it would keep him safe.

Sarah had been so proud when she found out that her dad's job involved working on real robots. In her eyes, it was the best job in the world. No doubt she imagined he was doing something much more interesting than sitting at a desk all day, staring at broken code. The only 'robots' he had any interaction with were unmanned drones, and the one that delivered coffee and snacks. Boy, did he love *that* robot.

"Aw, thanks, Sarah! I did almost forget! Maybe this thing will help Daddy make the alarms stop ringing?"

"Uh-huh!" She nodded dramatically, an enormous grin on her face.

"Well"—he kissed her on the forehead and tousled her hair—"I best be off, then. Love you!"

"Love you, too! Go fix the noises!"

He laughed.

"Have a good day." Cara kissed him on the lips one more time before he could finally leave.

"Why do you think I'm here?"

Kristopher Klein was in a foul mood. Terre had met up with the young man as they'd both strolled out of their homes and down the breezeway from the residential area of the base into the active area toward Intelligence.

Terre had made a comment about the need to quieten the alarms, which appeared to have agitated the young programmer.

They wouldn't get anywhere beginning the day at each other's throats.

"I just meant, I hope we can gain some headway today." Terre tried to justify his comments, despite not believing he had a need to. "Not that you haven't been trying."

"I've been in briefings and exercises since I stepped off the plane from California," K continued. "They can't expect a miracle if they won't let me work."

K's appearance was exactly how Terre imagined a lot of young computer programmers to look. A little disheveled; a little scrawny. His pale white skin hinted that he could have spent a few more hours at the beach. Even in the short time he had been on Guam, he must have had enough opportunity to hit the surf. He'd written K off as a gamer who didn't enjoy the outdoors. But he wasn't exactly out of shape—he must have kept active somehow. Though, he wouldn't be running a marathon anytime soon.

It bothered Terre that Kristopher didn't need to conform to the same military dress code as he did. For reasons never made clear to Terre, Andersen's XO—the base's Commanding Officer—had granted K an exemption from policy for his term on base. K sported both a ridiculous goatee and a shaggy mop of hair, and it was likely his contract wouldn't be long enough to make him shave either one. It shouldn't have, but it got under Terre's skin. Especially when Terre knew he would get razzed for his morning stubble.

He didn't know why it bothered him, as he wouldn't ever have worn his hair like that, anyway. He enjoyed being clean-cut and clean-shaven. His hand went to his face, feeling the roughness against his palm. Part of him enjoyed the feeling of making a small protest, but with the stubble being as rough as sandpaper, it made the rest of him itch. Terre would have taken the time to get rid of it if Fredricks hadn't lost his shit about silencing the alarms as soon as possible. '*No excuses,*' he'd said.

He better not complain about a little chin hair, then, Terre thought.

"I know," Terre replied, "but we've got to do what we can. I'm sick of these early morning wake-up calls. Let's see if we can figure this one out before oh-four-hundred."

"So much for getting a swim in."

"Would you really be going for a swim?"

"Probably not, but now I have an excuse not to."

As a contractor from NASA, and despite what he said, K wasn't only on base to fix the proximity detectors. Terre suspected that there was an additional need for an AI specialist to help diagnose some of Andersen's drone malfunctions. There were technological glitches happening throughout the base, many of which were never brought to Terre's attention, irrespective of his posting as Senior IT Specialist. The juniors usually had more AI training, on account of being great at spotting errors and making sure everything ran smoothly. Because the US Military outsourced the AI, there was no need for the best to be on base. Terre had his own issues with the most advanced military machines being contracted to the private sector, but he kept those concerns to himself. He had no influence in budgeting and the assignment of projects; he just made sure the computer systems stayed up to date.

But Terre knew something else was going on around the base; there had been whispers of an experimental program that was having its own difficulties. If Terre had to guess, K was here under a special program classified over his head, but it still would have been nice to have been brought up to speed. A little professional courtesy would have gone a long way.

Although technically on staff with the Central Intelligence Agency, Terre was more of an operating systems and network guru, specializing in network connectivity and managing day-to-day issues throughout the base. This AI Cloud babble had never been his repertoire.

Competition had been fierce for his position. The military wanted the best of the best, especially when war with a superpower was a possibility. And Terre was the best in his field. That wasn't his ego; it was just the cold, hard truth. When the biggest tech firms in the country bent over backwards to make you offers, you knew where you stood.

Only a few more months, and he would be ready to explore opportunities outside of government.

The alarm droned on in the background, too loud to be tuned out. But when lives were at stake, not being able to tune it out was the alarm's sole purpose.

The first couple of times it had sounded, everyone had gone underground, fleeing into the bunkers meant to protect them from an actual attack. Once it became clear the detectors were malfunctioning, Command had ordered for the response to be scaled back to standard precautions. Complete evacuation into the tunnels wasn't necessary. It was time-consuming and exhausting. Once or twice kept them well practiced; running away from specters in the night lost its appeal after that. They all had other things they needed to focus their attention on; other drills they had to run.

"Are you any closer to figuring out the issue?" Terre asked.

"I literally haven't had a chance to look."

Given the alarm was more tedious than it was practical, they strolled leisurely, which felt ironic considering the alarm would have the casual observer believe the world was ending. The humid Pacific air was bearable, the sun still just below the horizon and the breeze offering a sense of cool compared to the heat of the day. Terre took a deep breath, the smell of ocean air thick as it came in. If the alarm hadn't been drowning out all other noise, he'd likely have been able to hear waves crashing on the shore.

The ocean smell mixing with the permanent floral scent of the island always made him smile. Well, *almost* always. Even that wasn't enough to make Terre smile when the damned alarm started blaring at 3 a.m.

The narrow breezeway and its eight-foot-high concrete walls abruptly ended as they reached the principal center of the base. Once inside, it was clear that men and women were reacting to the noise, but only half-heartedly.

As the two technicians made their way to the Command Center, dozens of Airmen were, once again, getting into formation nearby. Their seamless march onto the Parade Square before the windowless buildings, keeping rhythm and formation even during these early morning hours, was formidable. It was a discipline Terre had never attempted to master. Even getting up for an early morning swim was an activity he'd never attempted to accomplish. Give him a late-night scotch on the rocks in a bar any day. The only good thing about mornings was a freshly brewed cup of coffee.

The blaring sirens muted the soldiers' marching footsteps, usually audibly pronounced during their early morning routine.

The discipline of the men was no less impressive than a typical morning, but Terre could tell that their hearts were no longer in the exercise. A dozen late-night false alarms made it difficult for the troops to remain enthusiastic. Chasing ghosts in the middle of the night left their reactions hollow, and they must have been running on little to no sleep. They didn't get enough on the best nights, but these sirens, every other day, were demoralizing.

"We're going to start getting used to going into work at 3 a.m.," he joked.

"I don't even know what time it is anymore," K replied. "I haven't had a chance to get used to Guam time yet. My brain still thinks it's nine o'clock in the evening." As if to emphasize his point, he stifled a yawn. "Still, it'll be fine. We'll get this thing taken care of and hopefully into a normal routine. Then I can focus on the drone malfunctions."

Terre arched an eyebrow at the revelation. It was the first time K had let slip that he had been hired for an alternative purpose. The two specialists hadn't exactly been close for the past couple of weeks. Their supervisors had K pulled away from his desk more often than Terre thought was necessary, and while K *was* at work, Terre mostly felt as if he were in the way.

"What's happening with the drones, anyway?"

K shrugged. "Some of them haven't been responding to commands. Central thinks there are bugs in the program. Always a bug somewhere. You need to brush up on your AI programming so you can give me a hand. The logic is the same."

Terre wondered briefly what NASA was doing differently to make this guy the expert they needed to bring in to fix their malfunctioning AIs. Surely the company that built the machines would have had some insight into the malfunctions?

"Not really my expertise, but I'm sure I'll need to go in that direction at some point. Anything we need to be worried about?"

The question was left unanswered as they stopped dead in their tracks. Terre nearly reached out to his companion for support as the earth abruptly shook. Two drones ripped overhead, a trail of smoke and light left in their wake.

"What the hell was that?" he asked.

All around them, soldiers had reached for their weapons, aiming blindly at the sky. They held their rifles at the ready, but there was no order to fire yet.

"*Air attack!*" someone bellowed into the night.

That sent the soldiers scrambling. Terre didn't understand the defense procedures on the island—he was only there to keep the servers running—but he knew they couldn't stay out in the open.

He looked over at his companion. Frozen in place, K's eyes were wide, looking to the sky, his mouth open. Terre grabbed him by the arm and dragged him forward. "Come on. Let's get to Central."

The ground shook again as a fireball billowed ahead of them. Terre stopped in his tracks and braced himself. Two more drones flew overhead.

"What the hell??"

He broke out in a run; damn Kristopher if he couldn't keep up. He called back to him. "Let's go!"

They were only IT staff; they had no way of defending themselves, although Terre doubted any hand-held weapons would do much good against an airstrike. Never mind that

Terre had never fired a weapon in his life. They needed to get somewhere that would provide cover. Some form of defense had to be better than nothing.

The command center was a few blocks away, but running straight for it would risk being caught in crossfire. Terre had no intention of allowing himself to be a target. Instead, they tried to stay as close as possible to the nearby buildings while still gaining some ground.

Terre had always known an attack was a possibility, no matter how remote the odds. The pay he was receiving reflected that. But it was always one of those abstract concepts he had thought would never happen. Now, chaos surrounded them.

Another explosion, somewhere Terre couldn't see, sent men and women scrambling toward battle stations. A plume of flame erupted as a missile found its target—a little too close for comfort. The blast lit up the night sky as a wave of heat passed over the pair of technicians. Much too close.

Lights soared overhead, the triangular shape of a drone, hovering far too low. Whoever was behind the assault, their intent was to destroy the base, or at least sow enough discord to render them inoperable.

The acrid smell of burning metal and oil stung Terre's nostrils. Whatever the missile's target had been, it had held fuel. Sirens rang out across the base, adding to the surrounding disorder.

"Move! Move!" a man's voice shouted above the clamor.

Additional men and women shouted in the distance, commanding orders in between alarms wailing in the night. The perimeter alarms offered a constant reminder of their own premonition, declaring *I told you so*.

A couple weeks of malfunctioning alarms had had them believing the network was crying wolf. With laser fire and explosions now all around them, it looked like the wolf had shown up.

Troops continued to aim their weapons at the night sky, some firing at phantoms. Then, as suddenly as the attack had begun, the sky grew quiet. Sirens faded into the abyss as men shouted at each other, trying to figure out where the targets of the attack were located, waiting for the next round of assault.

The two technicians didn't have far to go. Their brief run had closed the distance to their destination, and they hurriedly dipped through the doorway into the central command building.

"Hoffman! Kristopher!" a voice barked at them. "It's about time you showed up!"

Harry Fredricks was the CIA Technology Supervisor stationed on the island. His team were responsible for monitoring the Chinese and North Korean drone and AI programs. Recently, the two countries had invested a considerable amount of resources in AI research, and the US was trying its best to keep up.

"What the hell is going on, Fredricks?" Terre responded.

"No clue. I'm hoping you boys can help us figure that out. Set up in the Operations Center!"

"What's Intel picking up? Who's attacking us?"

"It's only been five minutes, Hoffman; the team are still scrambling for answers. Get inside!"

The three men sped down the hall into a sizeable meeting room. Glass walls surrounded the large Operations Center, and computers and projectors filled the open workspace. High-definition displays showed the positions of the drones, and lights flashed to denote incoming intelligence. Displays throughout the room flashed alerts amidst a strange red glow. A dozen men and women were running from console to console, trying to get a handle on what was going on outside.

Terre tried to read the updates flashing across the displays, but he couldn't make anything out aside from their level of importance.

"Status report!" Fredricks barked as they entered the room.

Nobody looked up, but one man shouted back, "The signatures are Chinese, but we haven't picked up any signals being sent toward them. It's almost like these drones are flying rogue."

"How many are we talking about, Trevor?"

The man at the nearest computer looked as if he was coming to the tail end of his night shift. Blood-shot eyes looked up at Fredricks as he shook his head. "There's only three."

Computers rattled and dust fell from the ceiling as another explosion hit outside. The drones were back for another round.

"Would the Chinese seriously launch an attack on US soil with only *three* drones?" Terre asked. "Seems like one hell of a pathetic way to drag us into a war."

"Which is why we think something went wrong in the programming on these units," Trevor continued. "We don't think they're being directed by anyone. They've launched on their own."

Fredricks crossed his arms over his chest. "Petrov's missile strike."

"Sir?" Trevor asked.

"In the 1980s, during the Cold War, a Russian computer system warned the officer on duty, Petrov, that a nuclear strike was on its way. He had to make the decision to inform his commanding officer whether to launch a counterstrike or not. But the system told him it was only five missiles. He thought the exact same thing as Hoffman just now—a pathetic way for America to start a nuclear war. He knew something was off; turned out to be a system malfunction." Fredricks paused, lifting a thick finger to his eyebrow, as if considering the weight of his next words. "Phone it through to the Pentagon before someone throws our arsenal at Beijing."

"Yessir."

"Wouldn't there be safeguards to prevent that from happening?" Kristopher jumped in.

"Our units have them," Fredricks answered. "God only knows what the Chinese have in place, but I'd like to think so. I sure as hell don't want to be the first line of defense in an all-out robot war. Accident or not, if we retaliate now, we guarantee that outcome."

The building shook again.

"Why aren't our guys taking these things out?" Terre asked, unsure if he had any authority to be asking questions.

"The units have somehow locked out our automatic controls. The enemy bots might not be receiving communications, but they're sending out jamming signals. We haven't been able to get our UAVs off the ground. We're relying on manned fighters."

"How is that possible? These are state-of-the-art machines. Our units should be shielded."

"I don't have enough information yet, sir. It's information classified above what we control on our level, anyway."

"Dammit!"

"We've taken out one unit so far, but we're working strictly with manual firepower, and the bulk of it is land-based. All automatic assistance is offline."

"Someone get me a phone. We're going to have to call Washington and find out what our next move ..."

Brick, metal, and a blast of fiery flame came rushing

through the room, blowing Terre backward and slamming him against a desk. He gasped as the wind was knocked out of him and he collided with the ground.

Muffled alarms echoed from outside, murky and thick, as though he were underwater. Thick smoke made his eyes water as Terre opened them, trying to get his bearings. Behind the smoke and dust that lingered, the night sky greeted him. Fire danced around the edge of his vision, and he put the pieces together.

One of the drone strikes had hit the command center.

Stars above him revealed that the attack had blown the roof clean off. Pieces of half-collapsed walls, their jagged edges licked by flame and smoky haze, revealed themselves.

He tried to move his legs. No luck. His arms and legs struggled as he tried to lift himself, wanting to have a look at what was holding him down, and the muscles in his core weren't responding properly, as if a weight resting on his torso was stopping him.

Terre gasped again. His lungs felt like they were on fire, making it impossible for him to suck in enough oxygen. Panic set in, and his body reverted to short, shallow breaths in attempt to take in more air. He was unable to breathe deeply, even if he wanted to. The pressure in his chest transformed into a stabbing pain, and Terre reasoned that it wouldn't hurt so much if he could keep the rise of his chest to a minimum. He struggled to keep his eyes open, his shallow breathing making him lightheaded, which didn't help to ease the terror that washed over him.

Stone, metal, and fire skirted the edges of his vision. The moon was bright overhead, taunting him, promising freedom that was just out of reach.

Gunfire surrounded him, and the ground shook as more firepower landed. Anti-aircraft fire rocked the base.

Through his blurring vision, Terre could make out a fireball rocketing through the sky. *At least one more down.*

"Help me get this off of him," Fredricks said, his voice distant, as if in a dream.

Where was Kristopher? Terre hoped the kid was okay. Within his first two weeks of K being contracted to the base, the sky had begun to fall, and now the kid was nowhere in sight.

"He's got half the roof on him; we need more men!" his supervisor's voice called out into the ether. It took Terre a moment to realize Fredricks was yelling about him. "You there! Jeffries? Send a few soldiers in here and then get to the medical center. You look like hell!"

"Hey, buddy!" Fredricks hovered above him and had raised the pitch of his voice, as if talking to a child, which told Terre that he must have looked like shit. Fredricks never took pity on anyone. Ever. "It'll be okay, Hoffman," he said. "We're going to get help."

"I can't move." Terre heard the words spoken in his own raspy voice. They were barely a whisper, and seemingly far away. He hoped this was a dream, and, with the way everything felt as though it were floating around him, it might as well have been. He closed his eyes and tried to will himself to wake up. No luck.

"Yeah, I know. We'll get you some help soon. Just hang in there!"

Terre sensed Fredricks leave, and never in his life had Terre so desperately wanted his loud-mouthed supervisor to stick around.

His vision was still fuzzy. Terre could sense movement around him, but he couldn't see any of it. Was this what dying felt like? Just drifting in an ocean of your own thoughts as the world rushed around you?

Why had those drones attacked the station? Things would get nasty if the assault drew America into a war.

Heat from a nearby fire crackled somewhere on the edge of his consciousness, followed by the sound of a fire extinguisher as it erupted nearby. Shouting. Running. Another blast of the extinguisher.

"… communications still jammed," said a voice in the distance.

"Kristopher, are you feeling up to having a look at …"

"My arm … I … can't … Are they still shooting at us?" Sobs and gasps punctuated K's words.

"Someone help me pull this desk off of his arm! Pull yourself together, Kristopher! We need to get in touch with …"

Groans came from both K and a few other men on the edge of what Terre could hear. What had happened to the kid?

"Okay … Okay … let me have a look," Terre heard him say.

"Someone get the kid's arm in a sling, and get him to a workstation! You're all right, Kristopher. Medic will fix you up in no time. I just need you to …"

Terre could hear choppers taking off in the distance. *Base Defense must have taken down all the drones*, he thought. The explosions had stopped as far as he could tell, but the world around him remained a cacophony of noise, most of it unintelligible to him.

"You're sure there aren't any more out there?" a commanding voice bellowed from somewhere in the distance.

"We aren't sure of *anything*, sir. Scans show the three that attacked us are down and our systems seem to be returning to normal, but your guess is as good as mine beyond that."

"Casualties?"

"It's too early to say, but one of those blasts hit the staff residences. It's not looking good, sir."

"Cara?" Terre whispered. "Is my wife okay? Sarah?"

There was no response.

He tried to cry out again, but all sound ceased. Tears, or blood—maybe both—ran down his face. Terre couldn't tell which; only that he was wet and, without the ability to lift his arms to wipe the droplets away, the liquid was dripping onto the floor beside him.

Everything faded and then went black as he finally lost consciousness.

Chapter Two

"That should do it," Dr. Judy Ballast said as she pulled the needle out of Terre's arm. "Your last nanobot injection. Give it a couple days before you go injuring yourself, but they should replicate on their own from now on."

Were it not for a few dozen monitors, robotic arms, and computer stations, Terre could have in been any other hospital room; as it was, he was currently recuperating in the rehabilitation center of the Treasure Island military base in San Francisco.

The attack on Andersen Air Force Base six weeks previously felt like another lifetime. A lifetime when his wife and daughter were alive and before the rogue drones had robbed him of his entire world.

For the past six weeks, he had lived with a lump in his throat, a hole in his heart, and a hoard of nanoscale robots swimming around in his bloodstream, allowing him to live on after the attack had dismantled his dreams.

Terre had struggled to convince himself life was worth continuing. Thoughts of suicide and death plagued his dreams. In the end, only the thought of fixing whatever malfunction had caused the rogue drone attack enabled him to keep going; to protect other innocents from suffering the same fate he had. But in order to work toward that goal, he had to fully recuperate first.

"Thank you, Dr. Ballast," Terre replied. He had to make a conscious effort not to rub his shoulder. Needles didn't bother him, but the size of this one had made him wince. "I'm surprised you didn't have the robot arm inject me this time."

"I've told you to call me Judy." She smiled, looking at him with her dark brown eyes and offering her sultry smile. He wished she didn't remind him so much of Cara.

"The surgical units have been giving us problems this week. We've got some guys from IT coming in to check them over this afternoon. Maybe you should stick around, have a look at them yourself?"

She sanitized the spot on his arm where he'd received the shot. In truth, the injection tingled more than it hurt. It almost tickled. He swore he could feel the microscopic robots moving inside his veins. After his first visit, his arm had been so itchy that he had been up half the night scratching it. Dr. Ballast had claimed it was psychosomatic; that he might feel some irritation due to the puncture site itself, but he wouldn't be able to feel the nanobots any more than he could feel a regular injection of fluid. Nevertheless, he'd woke up to a raw arm the next morning, so he had a hard time believing her.

"K would be a better choice for robotic equipment," he replied. Why did everyone assume that since he was in IT, he was a robotics expert? "Do you need me to come back for a follow-up appointment?" he asked.

"Well …" she began, as she disposed of the needle and removed her gloves, "you shouldn't need it, but as this is a fairly new procedure, I'd be interested in seeing you again in another week. I'd like to see how the nanos take to you."

"You haven't injected many patients with these things, have you?"

The doctor shook her head. "Military only, hun. You're one of six, including Kristopher over there. In some ways, you're lucky to have been as deep in the trenches as you were. Normally, staff don't get the experimental treatments."

"*Experimental?* That doesn't fill me with confidence, doc."

"Time will tell. There's already been an upgrade, so you'll be the last recipients of this particular batch. If you had been attacked now instead of six weeks ago, you'd be receiving an enhanced model."

"Oh? What are we missing? No security flaws, I hope?" K piped up from the adjacent table. K had previously expressed his initial concern that the nanos might be hackable. In his own words, he'd hate to become a 'walking bioweapon.'

"No security issues with this model. Just some overall enhancements. One treatment instead of six, for starters," the doctor said with a grin. Terre couldn't help but rub his arm. That would have been nice. "Plus, they've connected these little guys to the Cloud. New patients will get ongoing updates as they become available."

"Sounds handy. Why don't we get the upgrade?" Terre asked.

"Unfortunately, they aren't compatible with each other. We aren't sure why, but the two sets end up competing for dominance. Which means you're stuck with the older model until they find a patch."

"Wait—they've connected the nanos to *the Cloud?*" K asked. "If someone breaches the network, could they control these things?"

Dr. Ballast shrugged. "The Cloud is a secure military server. If someone gets into it, we've got bigger problems than someone messing with your cells."

K's glare was telling. "That's easy to say when they're not

your cells."

"Well, you're lucky you're getting the older models, then." She gave him a smile as she prepped the next shot.

Terre stood from the table and slid his navy t-shirt over his head. "Just as well," he said. "I suppose I'm lucky to have been able to receive the treatment at all."

"It saved your life, Terre. You owe these little bots everything."

He gripped the robot pendant that hung from his neck. "If only Sarah could say the same."

Ballast rested a hand on his shoulder. Terre gave her a half smile that didn't reach any deeper than his lips.

K was sitting up straight and taking deep breaths, pretending to not be nervous.

"Your turn, buddy." Terre slapped his friend on the shoulder, right where the injection would be going. "Last one, and you'll be immortal." K winced at the exchange, no doubt trying to assess if his shoulder was still sore from the previous five treatments.

"Well, not quite," Dr. Ballast answered. "While the nanos can heal pretty much any injury, they have limitations. Think of them as enhancing only what your body can already do." She had been through this all before, but Terre let her go through her spiel regardless. "They won't be able to repair brain damage—the neuron structures are too complex— although the upgraded models are supposed to have been showing some minor improvements in that area. Repairs are at a cellular level. If you lose a limb, they'll help you to heal it, the same as your body would, only faster. But don't go around thinking you're some kind of chameleon that can regrow a leg." She smiled to herself.

All the time the doctor had been speaking, Kristopher's face had grown three shades lighter; an impressive feat for one of the palest people Terre had ever met.

"All right, Judy, all right," Terre said with a chuckle. "You'd better give K his shot before he passes out."

He got a death stare from his friend. The man's dark black hair had grown significantly in the last couple months. They were supposed to be back at work tomorrow; hopefully, K had a haircut lined up before then, even though Terre had to admit that the shaggy mop and goatee seemed to suit his grumpy companion.

"Just get it over with." K's suddenly raspy voice matched his disheveled hair.

Talk about unlucky, Terre thought. *Contracted in from NASA mere weeks before the first ever drone attack on US soil. Some people just can't catch a break.*

Then again, none of them had had it easy.

K hadn't been as close to death as Terre, but part of a wall had fallen on top of his arm, completely mangling it. They'd put the poor kid on a workstation with one arm, trying to gain control of their own sensors. His body had suffered so much trauma and blood loss that he'd passed out in the chair. Once control of the base had been restored, both K and Terre had been loaded into an emergency Medevac helicopter where the nanobot treatment could be initiated. The same procedure had been followed for anyone else injured in the attack, though more had died in the attack than had survived. The nanobots might not have the capability to regrow a limb, but they'd got damn close with K's arm.

The two specialists had gotten to know each other a lot more in the time they had spent rehabilitating. K was bright beyond belief. Not only had he developed the proprietary software for the proximity detectors, but the kid had also designed some sort of AI project for the Mars colonies. The little he had shared with Terre over the past few weeks seemed fascinating, even though most of the project remained classified. During his stint with NASA, K and the team he had worked with had constructed a completely AI-controlled, self-sufficient settlement on Mars.

Terre longed for a challenge like that; to really test his capabilities. It was actually something he could look at being involved with, now that he was on his own again. There was nothing left for him on this planet, anyway.

Kristopher was still on the table, white as a ghost, as Dr. Ballast pulled the needle out of his arm and applied a bandage.

"Easy as pie, hun," she said, handing him his shirt. "Now, take it easy for a few days. Let the nanos adjust."

"That's the last one?" He looked at her, one eyebrow raised, the color returning to his cheeks.

"That's it. They'll take care of the replication on their own from now on. You're good for life."

"Sounds like I would have preferred the updated version," K whined, cradling the injection spot.

"Even with the Cloud updates?" Terre jabbed.

K eyed the needle he'd just received and bobbed his head, considering. "Maybe. Maybe not."

"Jonas, over there, received the new batch." Ballast pointed to a young recruit in a green tank top and khakis. The man was lying, unconscious, on a table in the next room, a panel of glass dividing them. "He just arrived here this morning. Drone attack in Honolulu."

Scars across the man's chest indicated a rushed battlefield procedure before the medics had shipped him out.

"Another drone attack?" Terre caught his breath as he said the words, fighting the mental images of the assault that had taken his family from him. The memory of flames, gunfire, and shouting were still fresh, echoing in the periphery of his mind. He took a deep breath to center himself; forcing his psyche to focus only on the here and now.

She nodded. "Sounds like it was under control pretty

quick, though. No deaths. Jonas got the worst of it. Broken femur; damaged ribs; punctured lung. But courtesy of the nanos we've pumped into him, he'll walk out of here tomorrow morning."

"They work that fast?"

"Yours will, too. They undergo six stages for your body to accept them. With the new model, we mix in a sample of the patient's blood, and the nanos imitate the molecular structure. The body hardly registers them as a foreign entity."

"Why didn't the EMTs do the procedure? It looks like they stitched him up before sending him?" In Terre's experience, he had always found the Emergency Medical Technicians of the US military to be fastidiously competent.

"We're the only facility that has access to the nanos. Like I said, they're completely experimental. The only reason we have them here is because we're just up the road from Silicon Valley."

"Have there been many attacks since Guam?" Terre asked. Hospital staff purposefully kept the patients out of the loop of anything that wasn't broadcast all over the news. And little had been leaked to the press, even about the attack.

"Command doesn't tell me much more than you," Ballast said. "I hear things once the bodies start coming, and we're far enough removed from the Pacific front to only see the fringe cases."

Before he could pry further, Terre's cell rang. His work phone. Back on call, it seemed.

"Hello," he answered.

"Hoffman!"

Terre cringed; only a handful of people called him by his last name, Harry Fredricks being one of them. He hadn't heard from the Technology Supervisor since the memorial. "What's up, sir?" he asked reluctantly.

"I know you're not technically back on duty until

tomorrow, Hoffman, but we need you. When you and Kristopher are finished in the infirmary, I want the two of you to meet me at the Intel Office. We've got some disturbing int that I want both of you to look at."

"Yes, sir. We're just finishing up. I'm feeling fine, by the way. Thanks for asking."

"Good. Ballast told me you were ready for duty." Terre's sarcasm was totally lost on Fredricks, mainly because he didn't give a shit. "Head over to the armory and get Matthews to suit you boys up. Things could get ugly real quick."

"Sir?"

"I can't explain now; we'll chat when you get here. I'll give Matthews the heads-up you're on your way. You're getting clearance *way* above your pay grade, Hoffman. Hell, it's above *my* paygrade. I'm talking experimental weaponry, but it's all precautionary. Move your ass." Fredricks hung up without further explanation.

Now that the kid was starting to relax after his shot, Terre could make eye contact with Kristopher. "C'mon," he said. "We're heading to Intel. Fredricks has something he wants us to see."

"Both of us?" Kristopher looked at him, wide-eyed. The kid had been shell-shocked since they had gotten back to San Fran, but then, no-one went into robotics expecting to have a building come down on them. *Although,* Terre thought cynically, *at some point in your career, you should at least consider that the day may come where they turn on you.*

He understood K's hesitancy. Hell, he had lost his entire family in the attack. He had tried to ignore the pain as best he could, but the numbness was irrepressible. His hand went to the robot pendant that still hung around his neck. Nobody had expected the attack on Andersen. Terre certainly hadn't. K had a right to be hesitant over heading back into the office.

"Yeah, both of us. Get that look off your face. Fredricks said he wanted us to *look* at some intel; no mention of us actually doing anything. It's probably just some techno-babble he needs translating."

Terre looked to the doctor. She had treated them well these past six weeks, and he had no complaints. When he had been told that he was getting the nanos, he had been expecting a cold and calculated experience. 'Alien probe' had been the first words that came to mind, but Terre was glad the treatment ended up being nothing of the sort.

"Thanks again for all you've done for us, Doc. I look forward to that follow-up visit next week." He shot her a sly smile and turned to follow Kristopher, who was already out in the hall.

The two IT specialists walked out of the infirmary and made their way outside. The Bay was ripe today: fish and sewage, mixed with the saltwater air, provided an especially putrid concoction. But San Francisco was as close to a home as he had, right now. It was nice to finally be on the mainland, somewhere Terre could find a decently priced latte or a top-shelf scotch—if he found a privileged bar whose suppliers still had stock of the drink. Pollution was the pits, but at least there was fresh coffee and no lack of events to help him escape his thoughts. Anything to keep the images of that night from creeping in.

The Bay had filled with cargo vessels that morning; shipping barges of all varieties, oil tankers, and even a few passenger ships had floated into port. Terre smiled at the few small sailboats that wove among them, getting an early start to what promised to be a beautiful July day. In between the sounds of the ships, he could just make out the sea lions barking at the wharf. Despite the cooler morning temperature, it appeared as though it'd be another day in paradise.

They made their way across Treasure Island, where they were being stationed. The name always made him smile. His home away from home for the past six weeks.

My only home, he thought as they crossed the cobblestone pathways that weaved between the repurposed buildings. He didn't really have anywhere else to go to, and between rehabilitating his injuries and coming to grips with the loss of his family, he hadn't been able to determine where he actually *wanted* to go.

The island sat halfway along the Bay Bridge, between San Francisco and Oakland. The Department of Defense had reclaimed the island a decade prior, as threats from across the Pacific had increased. Terre had barely realized the small artificial island existed, built for a World's Fair more than a century ago. It was separate enough for him to retreat into his own thoughts and not be disturbed by the greater buzz of the city, yet close enough to its amenities when he felt like emerging from the depths of his despair.

K turned to head straight for the Intel building. Terre grabbed him by the shoulder and pointed him in the opposite direction.

"What are you doing? Intel's that way," K asked, his voice still quivering. Terre realized that simply being called in was bringing back memories of the night of the attack. And how could it not? Fredricks had called them into his office, the two of them together. The sun was shining bright despite the early morning hour, but otherwise the situation was a bizarre mirror of events. It had apparently struck a nerve with K, and Terre couldn't say he blamed him.

"Listen," Terre said, "I know the attack in Guam was traumatic, but we made it. You and I—we're here, on good ol' US of A soil. And we've got these nanos working to keep us healthier than ever."

Whether they were, in fact, lucky in their fortunes was another question entirely.

"Yeah, and I was told I'd be maintaining servers, fixing a broken sensor, and monitoring drone deployments in Guam. Two weeks into that mission, I had to pull your ass out of a collapsed command center with a busted arm. Forgive me if I'm a little on edge."

"Glad to see you still have some spunk in you. Keep that edge but keep it under control. Whatever's happening, we're going to have to be able to work together."

"I know. I just need a bit of time to ground myself."

"Well, as much as I'd love to give it to you, we've just had six weeks' rest. We've gotta make do. Much as I'd like to mourn my family, I'm needed here. They've given us access to any military therapist we want; I suggest you take them up on that offer." Terre knew he was one to talk. *Do as I say, not as I do.* "But for now, they've cleared us to get back to work, and Fredricks wants our asses up there, pronto. He asked that we suit up first."

"*Suit up?* You mean, with guns? What for? Intel is a block and a half away! I'm a robotics contractor, not a soldier!"

"Hey, don't shoot the messenger!" Terre paused, his hands spread wide placatingly. "Especially not after we get the guns." He shot a self-amused grin and a wink over to K, hoping for a laugh. All he got was a scowl.

"Fredricks must have his reasons," Terre continued. "We'll see what's up when we get there. I'm just doing as I'm told."

Kristopher ran a hand through his hair. "I was in Guam under contract. And I only agreed to show up because they thought the sensor program I designed was acting up."

"Well, maybe they learned something. You heard Judy; Hawaii was just attacked. This is probably just a precaution."

"You better hope you're right."

Chapter Three

It was rare to arm staff and contractors, especially those that typically stared at code all day. The fact that it had been a special request from their boss, and specifically for the latest tech, had left Terre wondering. What bothered him even more was that it would have required top level authorization. Fredricks didn't have that kind of pull.

Terre wasn't as nervous as K, but that didn't mean he didn't wonder. His gut was telling him something wasn't right. Even though he had been formally out of the loop, he had still caught wind of several reports of drones going rogue and attacking bases since Guam. Sometimes they were foreign, sometimes domestic. It seemed every major country across the globe was having sporadic issues controlling their AI. Of late, there had even been an increase in the number of reports of civilian tech malfunctioning.

In the weeks that followed the attack on Guam, US Military Command had managed to de-escalate the fallout. Chinese drones attacking US soil would be world-ending, cataclysm level stuff if the public found out about it. It was hard to hide international distrust and high-level reports of malfunction, but somehow the most deadly details surrounding the events had been concealed. Leaks had led to the revelation of glitches present in the machines, but only the most hardcore of conspiracy websites had come close to guessing the extent of the situation,

Terre had only found out through others on the base that it had taken intense classified diplomatic negotiations and hard evidence brought forward for scrutiny to prove that programming glitches, and not ill intent, had been behind the recent attacks. The glitches being prevalent across all global AI units somehow allowed for cooler heads to prevail.

But that didn't mean the world powers trusted each other. Tensions remained high on both sides, with both the US and China skeptical as to whether the other would try to take advantage of the situation. The strain on international relations was impossible to conceal.

Terre had watched the filtered reports unfold on network news feeds. Internal tensions escalated alongside international pressure. Democrats and Republicans blamed the other for inaction while public pressure grew. It didn't help that '52 was an election year. Skepticism over the use of military AI units added to the larger automation debates; thousands of Americans were losing their jobs every day, and neither party seemed pressed to do anything about it. Terre rolled his eyes at the entire spectacle. He hated getting caught up in the latest news cycle, but there wasn't a lot for him to do on the island. His superiors wouldn't allow him to leave unsupervised as long as he was receiving the nano treatments.

He passed the time by running laps around the island, watching the news, and working out. K had spent the entire six weeks playing video games in the Commons.

"I'm just saying I wish I'd had a better look at the schematics." K had been going on about all the reasons to be concerned, but Terre had to admit he had tuned out most of what his colleague had been saying.

Seagulls cawed above them. Somewhere in the distance, a freighter blew its horn as it pulled into the bay.

"I've been here for six weeks, bored out of my skull, without even so much as the code to look at. Don't you think it's strange that the same malfunctions have been occurring in different units? Across different armies? Malfunctioning in twos and threes? They're all hooked up to separate Clouds. They have different software and hardware. It's just strange. If it were a bug in the software, you wouldn't expect both a Chinese bomber and an American cruiser to have the same malfunction. I also can't figure out why it only seems to affect a couple machines at a time."

"It sounds as though you've been privy to more intel than I have. Be thankful the entire fleet hasn't launched itself at once. What are you getting at?"

"I'm not sure. It's just weird. I don't know how to target the bug if I can't see a common thread connecting the anomalies."

"Could it be a virus?"

"Maybe, but I'd expect it to affect each of the units in the same way."

"Unless there's a randomizer built in? To make you think that."

"Perhaps, but that'd be one complicated piece of malware."

"Have you ever heard of the collective unconscious?"

"Vaguely. Isn't that the theory we unknowingly share parts of our psyche with the entire species?"

Terre nodded. "Carl Jung used it to explain how people on opposite sides of the planet came up with similar ideas at the same time. Like the crossbow, or the steam engine."

"So, what does that have to do with the drones? Are you saying the same design flaws were developed unconsciously by different developers?"

"Well, they're probably all based on the same fundamental programming languages."

"Yeah, but you know that's not how programming works."

"Or they've developed a collective unconscious of their own." Terre gave K a sly grin.

"Hah! You'd better hope not! But if your toaster starts to burn your toast at the same time as mine, you let me know."

Terre pulled the door open for K and let him enter the brick building first. The Logistics building still sported its original exterior, as built in the early 1900s; a true piece of American history. Inside, though, everything was different. Modern whites and greys, and not a spot of dust.

"Hey there," Terre announced as they walked up to the front desk. A young man, with skin a pastier white than K's and a bright blue streak through his otherwise black hair, sat behind a semi-transparent glass desk, a smart implant embedded in the side of his skull. Terre still needed to get used to these built-in cranial phone devices; he still opted for an old smartphone. He didn't even like the eyepieces most folks wore, preferring to keep the ability to put his device down when he was done with it. "Fredricks asked us to come here and suit up. He mentioned something about powered weapons? Maybe some phasers? I dunno. I'm supposed to ask for Matthews."

K shot him a look. "Powered weapons? You never said …"

"Names?" The receptionist interrupted K's protest.

"Terre Hoffman and Kristopher Klein, both spelt with a 'K.'"

"Sir?"

"Kristopher and Klein. Both start with a K. Fredricks ordered us here."

"Ah, yes, here we are. I'll get Samantha to take you to the equipment room." The receptionist tapped his keyboard a few times and looked back to them. "She'll be right out."

No sooner had he said the words than a tall woman with short red hair and wearing a grey suit and white blouse walked down the hall and approached the desk.

"Terre and Kristopher?" she said with a slight Southern accent. "Follow me, please."

Samantha led them down the hall. The building felt cold, sterile, and though it had clearly been renovated in the last hundred and fifty years, Terre could still feel the dank musk from the old building in his lungs as he breathed. The tiled floor was a glossy white, bright LED lighting giving the crisp white walls an otherworldly appearance. There wasn't so much as a shadow cast. For whatever reason, they wanted to keep these halls well lit. They continued through a series of turns and corners, and finally down a flight of stairs.

"Where are we going? Isn't the armory upstairs?" Terre asked, motioning toward the sign on the stairwell with an arrow pointing upward.

"The weapons Fredricks requested are Level 3 Classified. We keep them in a separate location."

She brought them into an open white room that lacked any differentiating characteristics, indistinguishable from the hall except for a long steel table and an armored door at the opposite end.

"Wait here. I'll bring them out." Samantha walked toward the door, pressed a button on a display panel, and a beam of light scanned her face before the door clicked open.

"What? We don't get to have a look at the rest of what you have in there?" K asked, eyeing up the doorway.

Samantha furrowed her brow and shook her head. "You only have clearance for a few items. I'll bring them out to you." She disappeared behind the metal door. Despite Terre's half-assed attempt to peer in after her, he couldn't see anything. Worth a shot, though.

"Why would *we* be issued classified weapons?" Terre

asked. "Nerds with guns doesn't sound like one of Fredricks's best ideas."

K shook his head. "I'm just a NASA employee. I have no weapons training. If I was told I'd be put in combat situations, I don't think I would have agreed to my contract. But hell, if I knew robots would have blown my workplace to bits, I wouldn't have come, either."

"I've never heard of IT reps being issued weapons before. I'm hoping it's just precautionary. But for what, I don't know. And why classified weapons?"

"Because they will be standard issue within a week or two," Samantha answered as she walked out of the back room. Her high heels clicked on the cold tile floor as she re-entered with an armful of weapons.

"Fredricks says he wants you equipped with them now, just in case we hit a worst-case scenario. He said you'll be working closely with the AI. If something goes wrong, he wants you protected."

"Protected from what?" Terre asked.

"I'll let him brief you. Right now, I'm just here to give you these." She held up two pistol-like weapons. With their sleek design and digital displays, they looked like something out of a science fiction movie. The pistols possessed a chrome-plated finish and a screen built into one side, and they were unlike any other firearm Terre had ever seen.

Samantha set down the pistols before swinging a metallic cannon off her back and onto the table.

If the pistols were unique, the second model was downright alien. Terre eyed the beast that lay on the tabletop. Essentially a two-foot-long chrome tube, the weapon possessed a deactivated, blue-tinted illumination band that circled its middle, broken only by a grip that protruded from both the top and bottom of the weapon.

"All right," Terre said, swallowing. "What are you giving us?"

"Cyber Dynamics's new tech line of high-powered energy weapons. There is nothing else like these on the market, and we have only used them in combat during a few missions."

"Cyber Dynamics?" Terre questioned. "They've really advanced their capabilities in the past decade if *they're* being awarded military contracts."

"They're essentially under our direction," Samantha replied, the corner of her red lips perked up in amusement. "What they showcase to the public is all smoke and mirrors."

Terre considered some of the tech he'd seen from the developer: a lot of cool gadgets, armor, and surveillance equipment that had been contracted to various city police forces. Nothing he had seen had resembled weaponry.

She held up one of the two weapon types she had brought out. It was large; definitely a two-hander. It looked like an elongated computer with a trigger.

"Don't fire this one unless you absolutely have to," she said. "The CD-52 Drone Surge, a portable EMP canon. NexGen3, so it's compact, but its charge is more permanent than the standard EMP explosion. It will disable any tech within fifty meters of detonation. If you're within that range, you'll even kill the weapon itself."

Terre had heard some of the theory behind NexGen3 technology, but only in passing. From what he understood, the charge generated by the device not only sent a one-time pulse through the blast area but also magnetized particles in the ground and atmosphere to continue releasing mini-pulses for an extended period of time, ensuring tech could not work in the area long after the initial detonation. The effects could last for decades, perhaps longer.

"Sounds useful."

"It's meant as a last resort if you have a drone—or worse —on top of you."

"Define *worse*."

"I'll let Fredricks fill you in on that bit. Just keep in mind you're only equipped with one shot on this bad boy, and you only have one to share between the two of you. If you fire it, you'll cost US taxpayers three hundred and fifty thousand dollars, so make sure it's worth it." She set the weapon down. "And spoiler alert—you're not worth that much, so you better be saving someone else's ass."

"Noted." Terre gave a sideways glance to K. He wasn't sure if he should be offended or amused. Horror filled K's face. Since he had no way of knowing what they were getting themselves into, Terre took it all in stride. Outwardly, at least. Inwardly, he was thrilled at being handed such weaponry. Usually at a desk all day, this was the sort of thing he only daydreamed about, like something straight out of a spy movie.

"A portable EMP weapon?" Terre raised a skeptical eyebrow. "Isn't a nuclear reaction required for that? What exactly is powering this thing?" He wasn't a weapons expert by any stretch of the imagination, but he knew that sort of output would require a lot of energy.

"Let's just say that information is above your paygrade. But this is all NexGen3 technology. We're not strapping a nuke to your chest."

K shot Terre a doubtful glance.

"So, fire this and the lights go out?"

Samantha nodded. "Yes, but the blast radius won't be more than a dozen yards. The CD-52 rounds are high concentration and meant to be used only as a last resort." You won't be able to see the blast, but you'll know if you hit your mark."

She forcefully pushed the Drone Surge into Terre's chest

and he grasped it, feeling the weapon's heft. Though it did have a bulk to it, the CD-52 wasn't arduously heavy, and he tentatively slung his arm through its harness, securing the firearm to his back and praying he'd never have to fire the thing.

Samantha kept going, seemingly ignoring the concerned glance Terre shared with K. "Next, we have your CD-115 Blaster Pistols. These are more your science fiction type weapons that fire laser bolts. Much more effective against a drone than bullets would be. Fry their circuits, if you hit them right."

"So, what's powering *these*? Or is that confidential as well?"

"Nanowire batteries. The newly patented model should last at least a thousand years, as long as they don't suffer any heavy damage."

"If I live that long, I'll let you know." Terre grinned.

"With those nanos they injected you with, it's improbable but not impossible, so I'd watch the snark."

"How do you know about those?"

"I'm in charge of tech inventory. Every piece of experimental tech in stock from here to Cheyenne is under my jurisdiction."

"So much for patient confidentiality," K said.

"Welcome to the CIA," Samantha answered.

She handed each of them a belt with the pistols attached.

"Don't burn each other's eyes out," she remarked. "I've got some other protective gear here for you boys, too. Vests, eye protection, and what have you. Most of it's just upgraded versions of what you're used to, so I won't bore you with the details."

"What we're used to?" K snorted. "I sit at a desk all day. I'm used to khakis and a polo shirt."

"Welcome to the big leagues, kid. Now, if you'll excuse

me, I've got some other work to take care of. I trust you remember the way out."

Terre nodded.

"Good. Don't go wandering anywhere you're not supposed to." She casually pointed to a camera in the corner of the ceiling. The warning was superfluous; Terre knew the entire base was under surveillance.

"Thanks for the tip."

"No sweat. Don't get yourselves killed."

Samantha left the room with a cursory wave, leaving Terre and K staring at each other, loaded with more weaponry than Terre guessed either of them had ever handled.

"What's her problem?" K asked.

"Who knows? After you've worked with the military a few years, you realize not to take things personally. Everyone is under a tremendous amount of stress."

"Now *that's* something I understand."

"C'mon, let's get going. Fredricks won't want to be kept waiting."

The two made their way to the Command Center. Once there, they found an eerie similarity to the night in Guam six weeks ago that even Terre couldn't deny. Fredricks hadn't been injured that night, but with the entire base in need of reconstruction, all non-essential personnel had been shipped to other locations. Since Fredricks oversaw IT, he got shipped with him and K to San Francisco. It made the most sense for him to be on hand to coordinate their expertise.

It was the first time the three of them had been in the same room together since the attack. The Intel Office looked nothing like the Command Center in Guam, but a security guard quickly escorted them through chasms of workspaces filled with displays, terminals, and lights. Most of the workers were silent, heads down, working away on projects Terre could only catch snippets of, other than a few officers intensely chatting in hushed tones. Terre saw more than one pair of hands lifted to rub a temple or tired eyes. The level of tension in the room was palpable.

"Welcome back, boys!" Fredricks's eyes lit up as he entered the room.

"Miss us, sir?"

"You're damn right I missed you, but don't get sentimental. While you two science experiments have been waiting around, we've been trying to get this situation under control." Fredricks stepped up to the nearby elevator and hit the 'up' button.

"Glad to see you're up and about, too, sir."

"Don't get cute. Have a look at this report we got in this morning from Intel in Shanghai." Fredricks planted a manila folder in Terre's hands. *Looks like we're going back to printed notes*, Terre thought.

They stepped into the elevator, and Fredricks hit seventeen on the panel.

"Drone attack on a Chinese military base in the South China Sea," Terre said, scanning over the report.

"If the malfunctions were the same as at Vanuatu, this would be simpler," stated Fredricks. "But this attack was orchestrated by their own units. Their own drones decimated the base."

It hadn't made the news, but Terre had overheard a few conversations at the gym around the subject. Similar to the events in Guam, an attack on Chinese forces in the middle of the night the week prior had caught the PLA forces off guard. China had kept tight-lipped about the event, not wanting it to leak that they were having their own encounters with rogue AI.

"So why bring us in? K hasn't been able to get started yet, and from the gossip I've heard in the locker room, this isn't the first time drones have attacked a friendly base, is it?"

"I wish that was the worst of it. Come sit down in my office."

Terre and K followed Fredricks into the spacious office. The window behind his desk provided a beautiful view of the Bay.

"Not too shabby." Terre pointed to the window as Fredricks gave him a questioning glance.

"You never tire of it, either. Room—close blinds."

The computerized blinds closed, and the room darkened. Fredricks hit a button on a remote control, and a projector whirred to life.

"Voice controlled blinds, but the projector's still operated by a remote?"

"Don't get me started." Fredricks rolled his eyes. "Brand new building, but they still decided to cut corners on the IT equipment. They could have used your help here months ago."

"Funny. Like anyone has ever considered *my* advice for equipment purchases," Terre chuckled.

"Go figure. It'd make *too* much sense to get the input of those actually using the tech."

Fredricks turned the projector on, and a title screen bearing the CIA and US Department of Defense logos lit up the screen. The text read: *United States of America Robotics Defense Program—Classified—Level 3.*

"I don't need to tell you boys that nothing you see here gets discussed outside of this room, unless absolutely unavoidable. And by *unavoidable*, I mean you have one of these suckers staring at you with a finger on the trigger.

These are slides that, under normal circumstances, we would never have authorization to see."

He alternated the slide, and an image of a standard militarized drone filled the screen; graphite armor and control light accents decorated its frame. "This should be familiar to you, Hoffman," Fredricks said, pointing to the screen. "The jewel in the crown of the military's robotics program. Droids sent into the line of fire to disable mines, conduct intelligence ops missions, and to control bombers and aircraft remotely."

Terre nodded. He was astutely aware of the program, having worked adjacent to it every day for the last two years. The concept wasn't particularly well understood by the public, but it also wasn't exactly classified, either.

Fredricks continued. "Except those are only the ones Command tell us about. R&D has been working on a highly classified advanced line for nearly a decade now. Unfortunately, we picked the wrong time to bring them online."

"Sir?"

"We'll come back to that, but first you need to be aware of what we've created."

He flipped a slide, and an image of a humanoid robot filled the screen: a combination of bone-white synthetic skin mixed with what looked like a type of graphite armor and control light accents that decorated its frame.

"What you're looking at is an example of a US Sentinel B-class unit. Built for combat, security, and control."

"A war machine. How did those get approved?"

"Command passed them off as a supplement to the National Guard. In an emergency, these fellas would barricade roads and escort people to safety. They're also programmed to take out enemy targets if directed to or if a threat is detected. They are fully capable of using Level 3 energy weapons, such as the ones we have outfitted you with, and they are highly efficient in hand-to-hand combat."

"So, we've created a Terminator."

"Try tens of thousands of Terminators."

"What could possibly go wrong?" Terre rolled his eyes.

Fredricks changed the slide, ignoring the remark. Three glossy orbs appeared on the screen: one white, one gray, and one jet black, which was much larger than the others. "These are our next level drones. Top level magnetic lift technology. Their bullet- and explosion-proof exteriors double as display readouts. Useful in hostage or emergency situations where we need to provide additional instructions."

He flipped the slide again, and a video started playing on the white drone's surface, showing a potential evacuation route. Useful if it was trying to help a hypothetical person in distress.

"All models are purpose-built for these protocols, except for the Onyx model. The Onyx"—Fredricks pointed to the larger orb—"are our black ops units, built for covert strikes. The unit fires laser bolts strong enough to vaporize a nearby target."

Terre studied the units. With their glossy glass exteriors and displays that surrounded their spheroid bodies, they made him think of a ball-shaped smartphone.

"Sir, as interesting as this is, I hope this isn't leading where I think it is."

"Patience, Terre. I'm showing you this so that you understand what the USA has in its inventory."

"I've seen these before," Kristopher said, jumping in. "These are similar to the units we deployed to Mars for terraforming."

"They're the very same, actually. The program repurposed the Mars bots and reprogrammed them with military functionality."

K shook his head. "The Mars units were programmed for colonization. Their sole purpose is to protect the colonists from an uninhabitable world. They're meant to help until we can complete the terraforming process. I wrote a large part of the program myself."

"And that's why you're still here, Klein. We need you."

"I'm not sure I understand. Is there a programming issue? Why not bring in whoever installed the military application?"

"Kristopher, there is no person in this country, maybe on this planet, that understands these Artificial Intelligence programs better than you do. We have what we need right here."

Fredricks had deftly avoided the question, but K was too taken aback by the compliment to notice.

"I guess that's what I signed up for. I've been begging to do something useful for the last few weeks."

How quickly his tune changes when you pay him a compliment, Terre thought.

"The Chinese lost control of their units late last night. Their drones attacked the Yulin Naval Base, wiping out any ability they had to retaliate. At first, the Chinese blamed us for hacking their units. The only problem is, we lost control of our robotic units roughly two hours after they did."

"Which robotic units?" Terre winced as he asked, afraid he already knew the answer.

"*All* of them." Fredricks flashed them a glare to let the repercussions sink in.

"Including these classified units?"

"Precisely."

"Have there been any further attacks on US facilities?"

"Not by these units. Or not yet, at least. But we're not ruling anything out. We've had our team trying to connect with the units all night."

"Can't we just pull the plug? Take them offline?"

"We can and have done that, with no response. We're currently working with other countries in an unprecedented, coordinated effort to facilitate an override."

"And the new units?"

"The new units are a little trickier. They can run for months without needing to recharge, and the only way to disconnect them from their internal power source is to manually dismantle each one."

"How long will that take?"

"Too long. We've got a hundred thousand Sentinel robots and another twenty-five thousand orbs on inventory."

"What the hell were you people thinking? A *hundred thousand* units?" Kristopher was on his feet, perplexed by the sheer scale of the escalating situation.

"Do you know how many disasters due to global warming the US military has had to respond to across the country in the last half-century alone? *Thousands*. And not a single one of them demonstrated that we had enough personnel to respond effectively. Every year, the disasters get worse. Throw in a pandemic, like that Covid shit thirty years ago, or North Korea deciding to fire a live nuke at us, and we'd be all out of options. These Sentinels are the answer to having enough boots on the ground to cover the fifty states, plus all our protectorates."

"So, what now? We destroy the lot of them?"

"That option is on the table, but only as an extreme last resort. We have tens of trillions of dollars invested in these things. If we can salvage them, that's our priority."

Kristopher had his head in his palm as he listened. "Are you still able to access them via the Cloud?" he asked. "Have you tried wiping them?"

Fredricks shook his head. "There are too many safeguards. The number one roadblock we had in getting the funding for these things was the fear they would be hackable. The Sentinel operating systems have been designed to resist brute force protocols. Anything that appears foreign to their systems, or any attempt to wipe them, and they'll immediately lock us out and default to combat mode."

"So, there's no access to the network?"

"There are several access points that are still pinging back positive. The team thinks there's a slight chance we could get something through. But there's also a good possibility the Sentinels will shut down anything they don't recognize and close the remaining live connections. In effect, we've got one shot."

"*Great*." Kristopher sat back down, grabbing his unkempt hair.

"K?" Terre asked. "You okay, buddy?"

"*Okay?* How can I be okay? Do you realize what he's saying?"

"Yes. Killer robots. Surely there's a safeguard for this sort of thing?"

Fredricks pursed his lips and sat down. "R&D put safeguards in place to prevent an enemy hacker from taking them over. But we have no provisions for them locking us out on their own."

Terre stood up, wide-eyed. "You're telling me that not *one* of our roboticists had seen a science fiction movie where killer robots gain consciousness and turn against us? There wasn't a provision built in for that?"

"Look, I'm just passing on the information I've received from Command. Calm down. From everything we can assess, these robots aren't conscious. Their actions are a result of the programming they follow. But something has temporarily locked us out of their controls. If you lose control of your robot vacuum, the only thing it's able to do is clean the carpets."

"Except we're not talking about vacuums, are we, Fredricks? The only things that murderous war machines are programmed to do is to *destroy* us. Fantastic. Well, I'll take comfort in knowing they aren't aware of what they're doing."

Fredricks didn't look impressed at Terre's disparaging tone, but he chose not to say anything.

"Why are *we* here?" K glanced up at Fredricks, contemplating something. "Surely you have internal specialists who have much more experience with the design? Hell, why aren't you speaking with the developers who manufactured the units? Why bring in your network guy and a contracted employee to help? What aren't you telling us?"

Fredricks tapped his fingers on the desk, hesitant about the words he was about to say. The projector above their heads hummed as the image of the Sentinel robots remained illuminated on the screen before them. Its appearance resembled something out of a horror film. Its blue eyes were vacant, the white synthetic flesh wrapped around its face attempting to simulate the look of a human. It was the absolute definition of the uncanny valley; a machine worked down to the very detail of trying to appear human, and yet still appearing far more creepy than comforting.

"I'm hoping," Fredricks said, his voice low and measured, "you'll have an idea as to how we can bring these things back under our control. Or, at the very least, how to prevent a hundred thousand robots from attacking our citizens. Our internal teams are fresh out of ideas. They're too afraid to send any data up the stream blindly and risk being locked out altogether, and I can't say I blame them. We brought you in because you were involved in creating the Mars program. R&D built the bots' programs on top of your own, and Command is hoping you'll have some insight into the original systems that they've overlooked. Hoffman, as one of our network specialists, is here to apply that logic across the estate."

"How much time do we have?" K asked, trying to calculate something. What he had in mind, Terre wasn't sure.

"Not long."

Chapter Four

"So, these things are completely unhackable?" K had managed to grab the projector remote and was bouncing back and forth between slides, studying each one intently. Images of bots danced from one slide to the next each time K tapped the device.

Fredricks stood at the head of the long table. He had removed his suit jacket and had hung it over the back of his chair, revealing the breadth of his chest muscles. Terre had never realized the man was built like a tank. Sweat marred the edges of Fredricks's armpits—despite the room not being warm, the heat of the situation was getting to him, and Terre knew it wasn't like the man to stress easily. "Like I said, at most, we have one shot at getting this right."

"But if the units detect foul play, they'll sever the connection and automatically activate?" K confirmed.

"Correct."

"Do I need to ask what happens once they're activated?"

"Probably not."

K rubbed his temples.

"Why is that the default?" Terre asked. "Why would they instantly activate and start shooting? It doesn't make any sense."

"I'm guessing that's not what would happen in a normal scenario," K answered, still staring at the screen. "The units would be programmed to turn on, alert Central Command that there has been a breach, and then await further orders. If something affected only one machine, Central would probably isolate it from the rest of the network. It's only a problem when we're no longer the ones giving the orders. If the machines have somehow taken control of their own programming, they'll go about doing exactly what they were programmed to do." The IT specialist looked to Fredricks for confirmation, who simply nodded and cleared his throat.

"But what does that mean, exactly? What are we dealing with?"

"If we were talking about the bots my team deployed on Mars, they'd probably continue to grow vegetables, monitor the colonists, and proceed with terraforming the planet's surface, getting it ready for human life. They'd ensure there were sufficient resources for the colonists. There are no weaponized protocols up there."

"But these machines were built for war." Terre said, putting the pieces together. "If our attempts to interface with the network trigger a failsafe, we risk waking them up and having them all go into attack mode?"

"Precisely."

Fredricks was pacing slowly back and forth across the room, his hands held behind his wide back. He was being incredibly patient as the two technicians talked things through. This was not his normal behavior. Was he being considerate because Terre had lost his family? Or had something changed because he had witnessed an entire military base being vaporized? Either way, it was a welcome change to the barking they'd normally have received by now.

K turned to Fredricks. "One more time. If the safeguards are in place to recognize a foreign program, why bring *me* in on this?"

"It's safe to say we're desperate. You wrote the program

for the NASA bots. You know how their systems are designed."

"Who modified the programs for military use? DARPA? Surely they can figure out what's going on?"

"They've gone as far as they can. They're hoping the problem is rooted deeper in the code."

"Of course."

"Look, if there's a way we can take these things down without having to rain down NexGen EMPs on American cities, we need to find it. The Pentagon is breathing down my neck over the fact we've lost control of these things in the first place. This might end up being the worst disaster the world has ever faced, and I, for one, am not ready for it to be on my watch. I know what I'm asking of you is outside of your normal job description, but we don't have any better options."

K stood up from his chair, his eyes still fixed on the screen. "Were the machines built from the same schematics as the NASA units?"

"I believe so, yes. It's all included in the binders on the table."

K grabbed a binder, sat back down, flipped it open, and continued. Terre could tell K was in his element now; that this was where his confidence could finally shine through again.

"What about the Sentinels? They look different from anything we designed. There's no need for that sort of intimidation on Mars."

"The bodies were redesigned and the units were given original command settings, but the core coding is the same as the caregiver units you have on Mars. What are they called? The babysitter bots for the scientists' kids?"

"We call them the Keepers. But it's a hell of a leap from childminding protocols to military application."

"You'd be surprised. The units were designed to be instinctive, dexterous, and quick thinking," Fredricks replied. "The modifications for military use are not as substantial as you'd think."

"Got it." K had flipped to the Sentinel section in the binder, studying it as if it might hold the answer to whatever question he was mulling over.

"How do we know the AI haven't completely shut down access to the network already?" Terre chimed in.

"We're still able to ping the connection. If they'd locked us out, we wouldn't get a response. Granted the pings are more limited than they should be, but we're not out of the game yet."

K still had a distant look in his eye, but he was sitting up straight, his shoulders back. This was his domain. Terre had seen that look from him before. K had an answer. He was simply working through the variables before sharing.

"Structurally, the orbs are the same units as the Mars project but with an upgraded program. The Sentinels have a base programming fundamentally the same as the ones I designed at NASA. Is there a chance the units won't detect an attempt to override their new military programs if we try at the code's base level?" K asked.

"If *you* don't know, *I* sure as hell don't," Fredricks shot back, his old, agitated demeanor returning. "Gentlemen, right now, there is only one person alive who is capable of pulling that rabbit out of their ass, and I'm looking at him. Figure out whatever plan you think could work. I'll authorize any hair-brained scheme you think has a one-in-a-million shot. But if it doesn't work, we may be looking at the end of modern civilization."

K visibly swallowed. *No pressure, buddy.*

Fredricks's cellphone rang. He looked at the display,

raised one finger towards the two men, and stepped out of the room to take the call.

"What are you thinking?" Terre asked K once they were alone. "I can tell you've got an idea."

"The systems are designed to prevent foreign code from being installed. Uploading any sort of virus or hacking their program is impossible. But what if we could reinstall the code that was there originally?"

"The NASA programming?"

"I'm wondering if the units would accept the original code as an update to the operating system. There's enough of the original coding there that the alien signature protocol might not be triggered. The programs are compartmentalized. Newer code won't affect most of the base systems, and the sequences that would be overwritten would still have the proper crypto-signatures. The operating system might not interpret it as foreign."

"Kind of like a system reset."

"Yes."

"Sounds simple enough. Turn them off and on again. Occam's razor. I like it. But what if we do that and we still can't control them?"

"Well, if they don't lock us out first and we can restore the original program, we'll have uncontrollable robots designed to protect a human colony on Mars instead of uncontrollable war machines intent on blowing Earth to shit."

Terre crossed his arms and nodded. "Gotta admit, that sounds slightly better."

"There are a few other sticking points that could throw the whole thing for a loop, though. Tweaking the code would wipe out the bots' weapons protocols, which sounds wonderful in theory, but I honestly don't know how the systems will respond when the upload tries to wipe that part out."

"Right. You're thinking the military programmers might have installed a separate signature for those protocols?"

"I think they'd have had to, but I have no way of knowing for sure without being able to look at the program. And even then, it would take weeks."

"Okay. What else?"

Kristopher cycled through the slides on the projector to one of the orbs: the large black one with blue lights dancing around its screen-like exterior.

"This isn't one of the original machines; its schematics are entirely different. There's core similarities, of course, but that's about it. Kinda like Piccasso and Monet; both use paint, but what they do with it is completely different. These orbs are built entirely for war; they have no other purpose. The military have taken our terraforming machines, beefed them up, and turned them deadly. These could bring the whole plan down. Even if they don't … I don't know what kind of effect, if any, the old program will have on them."

Terre nodded, digesting everything K had laid out for him. "So, if this works, it's just going to be our machines, right? This won't have any effect on the international units? China? North Korea? They're still going to have issues, right? Could this all come back to haunt us?"

K bobbed his head, considering. "Yeah, but I don't know how we get around that. For now, let's take this one step at a time. If this works, maybe we can help the rest of the world to follow suit."

Fredricks burst back into the room. "We've got to act now, boys. I hope you have a plan."

"I've got an idea," K answered. "It's a long shot, but I don't think we have any other option."

"Great. I just got word from the Pentagon. These drones are on the move."

"What do you mean?"

"Those black orbs." Fredricks motioned to the image still projected on the screen. "The Onyx. Some of them are flying this way."

"How many?"

"It sounds like two for now, but there are hundreds more where these came from. And we don't want to find out what happens if they start an all-out attack."

Terre couldn't help his jaw from falling to the floor. He had already lived through one drone assault, and that had been devastating enough. Now, there were classified war machines heading to an area that housed millions of civilians. What was worse was that their fate suddenly appeared to be in his hands. This wasn't what he had signed up for.

"Wait a minute. What exactly are we dealing with here?" Terre asked. "This is going to be Guam all over again."

"This will be far worse than Guam," Fredricks answered. "These units were built with the most advanced technology on the planet. They fire energy weapons that can level buildings. Let's just say this could be the end of San Francisco."

"Couldn't Command authorize a localized EMP charge over these units? Take these two out before they reach the city? If nothing else, it could buy us some time." Terre wasn't a weapons specialist, but the idea made sense in his head.

"The Onyx design includes standard EMP shielding. A standard electromagnetic pulse won't do anything to these things. There isn't time to bring the weapons needed online before they get here, and the blasts need to be deployed from NexGen3 tech. We don't have time to get into specifics, but the effects are far more permanent than a regular burst. We fire one of those, and a good chunk of San Francisco won't be able to operate technology of any kind for hundreds of years."

Terre opened his mouth to ask a question about the tech, but before he could get a sound out Fredricks raised a hand, preempting Terre's questions. "No specifics, Hoffman. Suffice to say, if there *was* another option, none of us would be in this room right now. K, you have the floor. Fill me in on your plan."

"I'm going to upload the original NASA Guardian Program, with the goal of resetting these things back to their original state. If we reset the units to NASA protocols, maybe it will stop them from shooting at us, at least."

Fredricks nodded, his lips pursed as though considering. "You don't think their current program will have a timestamp or critical dependencies? The differences won't shut the whole upload down?"

"For every upgrade we do, there has to be a way to rollback in case a patch does something we don't expect. It's likely the same on any of your server upgrades. There are going to be an insanely high number of revisions from the time the modifications started, but essentially, it'd be like restoring from a backup. It's the only idea I have, so if you have something better, I'm all ears."

The image of the Onyx loomed over them from the projector screen. Terre had a hard time breaking his gaze from the computerized sphere. It was so unlike any other technology he had ever seen at the base.

"Obviously I don't," Fredricks said. "I just sure hope you're right. Gather what you need. I'll make the arrangements for the upload."

"All right, then. Let's go." K got up and headed for the door, suddenly filled with a confidence and determination Terre hadn't seen in the kid since Guam.

"Where exactly are we going?" Terre asked.

"My office," K replied. "Silicon Valley."

"Be quick. The Governor has already issued a state of

emergency, and the President's going to order a national lockdown. Try to get through before the blockades are in place. Your credentials will get you through, but the highways are going to be murder."

Terre and Kristopher left the building and made their way through the parking lot. K wasn't waiting; he was practically running.

Terre jogged a few steps before slowing his pace. "Hold up, K!"

Kristopher stopped in his tracks, turning around. "Are you kidding? You were in that meeting, right? They're headed this way!"

"I was, but I'm not running to Silicon Valley. Get in the car."

K lifted his ear to the sky, scanning for something. "Do you hear that?"

Terre stopped and listened. He heard the bellow of a freight ship laying on its horn; the grating sound of seagulls cawing all around them; jet boats buzzing in the harbor. Typical sounds of San Francisco on a July morning.

He shook his head. "I don't hear anything."

K stood still, eyes to the sky over the city. Terre followed his gaze over the Bay Bridge into San Francisco.

Then he saw them.

In the distance, two menacing black orbs hovered over the sea, on a course toward the city.

"Those are the weaponized ones, right?" Terre asked.

K nodded and ran his hand through his black mop of hair. "Shit, Hoffman. There's nothing we can do about those two reaching the city. This is going to take time."

"It's bad enough Fredricks calls me that. Don't you start."

"Sorry."

"The quicker we can get there, the less damage they'll be able to cause. Come on, we've got to get to …"

Intense blue light ejected from one of the orbs, blasting into the middle of the Golden Gate Bridge. The roadway crumbled into the bay as its red towers fell inward, erupting in a wave of metal, concrete, and water below.

Terre's mouth fell open. *"Shit!"* He broke out into a run and regretted berating K for doing the same a moment ago.

Terre tried not to look, but it was impossible to avert his eyes as the iconic landmark fell into the sea. From his vantage point, he could make out both cars and people tumbling into the bay. Debris was airborne, landing on vehicles indiscriminately. Horns, though at a distance, were audible as they echoed off the water's surface. The noise garbled and then silenced as the cars were washed away.

"We've gotta get out of here before those things take out the Bay Bridge as well!" Terre shouted.

"You think I don't know that?" K yelled back.

The parking lot wasn't big, so they covered it in a matter of seconds. They hopped into Terre's gray four-door hatchback. A robot medallion hung from the rearview mirror; another keepsake of his daughter's that he'd salvaged from the wreckage of their home. He unconsciously grabbed the matching pendant that hung from his neck.

He turned off the car's autonomous mode and navigation guidance—Terre would be the one driving today—and punched the car into Drive. The stereo sprang to life, and the sound of the Foo Fighters playing an old song from the turn of the century drowned out all other noise as they sped through the base, making their way onto the exit ramp that led toward the Bay Bridge.

K wrinkled his nose as he turned the volume down on the

touchscreen controls. The car itself was silent, and the distant sound of sirens replaced the music.

"What the hell are you listening to?"

"I like the old stuff," Terre said. "Real singers, real instruments."

"This is what my grandpa listened to," K said.

"I don't think my taste in music is our biggest concern right now. How do we get to your office?"

"Best bet will be to go through Oakland, head south, and circle back to the Valley." K had his eyes skyward. "Let's steer clear of the city if we can help it. Right now, I'm betting that heading away from the crazy bots is a better plan than heading *toward* them."

A shadow flew overhead. The pair couldn't help but watch. Terre also tried to monitor the bridge and the ramp ahead of them.

Terre looked from east to west, trying to assess their options. "Everyone's going to be trying to get out of San Fran," he said.

He tried to get a look at the flow of traffic to see if he could pull the vehicle in somewhere. There was no way that was happening, though; the bridge was already slammed with people trying to flee the city. *That didn't take long,* he thought.

"We're never going to get through that!"

"You don't need to shout; I'm in the same vehicle," K said, rubbing his ear with a look of disgust on his face. "Look, don't panic."

K was telling *him* not to panic? *Great.*

"Okay. What do you suggest?" Terre asked.

"We've got to circle back."

"What? But you just said ..."

"Just go! Hurry!"

Terre shook his head. If K thought he was going to boss

him around … He put his foot on the accelerator and whipped the car around, facing toward the heart of San Francisco. This was suicide, but unless they wanted to sit on the bridge for who knew how long, it was their only option. If those bots took out the bridge before they could cross it, it would mean death all the same.

The upper part of the bridge which led into the city was wide open. It surprised Terre that nobody was trying to make it out of the city by going the wrong way. *Still time for that, though*, he mused. The carnage had only just begun, and he guessed most people hadn't even had a chance to digest what was happening.

Ominous black plumes rose in the distance, marring an otherwise perfectly blue sky above the harbor. The NASA office was an hour away, and the black orbs were still circling the city. What had they gotten themselves into?

"There's no chance you have this program you need on the Cloud somewhere, is there?"

K shook his head, his face glued to the window. "It's all on internal systems. Space program secrets. There was no need to access it outside of the office. There's one link in Florida, but it's a closed network. Sorry; using a space program to stop a bunch of killer robots never really crossed my mind."

"Well, next time, maybe you'll consider it." Terre earned an unimpressed eye roll, but he laughed at his own wit. Somehow, he felt the urge to break the tension brought about by the impending war machines descending upon them.

The top deck of the bridge was clear. A few drivers had pulled over to the side of the road. Terre watched a dad holding his kid and pointing at the carnage happening on the other bridge across the bay. He lay on the horn.

"Don't stop on the bridge!" he yelled as he swerved.

Terre grunted and hit the accelerator. The guard rails

separating the road from the icy bay beneath seemed endless. *You don't realize how long the Bay Bridge is until you're trying to cross before robots destroy it.*

A chopper rose from the middle of the city and banked over the Bay. Whether they were reporters, police, or military, Terre couldn't tell, but he hoped the local news networks wouldn't be stupid enough to send their reporters up with those orb-shaped drones firing upon the city. The chopper whirred toward them, heading toward Oakland; possibly trying to make a wide arc around the city to get a better look.

Definitely the news. Idiots.

The *KGO7 News* logo was prominent as the chopper flew ahead of them, following the bridge. At least it wasn't trying to get closer to the orbs. Though Terre didn't doubt they were having that conversation in the cockpit.

"Should have used a helicopter," K said, eyeing the chopper as it flew past them.

A blue burst of light lanced over them and struck the *KGO7 News* team. Terre jumped as flames erupted from the chopper, causing it to fall from the sky, right into the middle of the Bay Bridge behind them.

"Maybe not."

The bridge shook violently, and Terre had to maneuver to keep the car in their lane. Horns and alarms erupted all around them. The city was going to crumble before they even made it off the bridge.

Glad we didn't go the other way, he thought. Would those on the bottom deck of the bridge even know what had happened? A split-second decision by K had saved them. He looked at the young technician, his eyes still glued to the sky.

Terre hit the gas as they reached the end of the bridge and raced into the city. Framed in his rearview mirror, the now-redundant news helicopter sat in the middle of the road, engulfed in flames. Two people rolled out of the aircraft. He couldn't believe that anyone had survived that, but somehow, they had.

It was a short-lived victory. The car shook once more as the flaming bridge let go of its supports and collapsed beneath the chopper, and the roadway fell into the Bay. Just like that, the AI-powered orbs had cut off San Francisco from its neighbors. The only access to the city was now to the south.

As Terre and K entered the city, skyscrapers on their right blocked out much of the smoke rising from Golden Gate Park. The bright blue sky above them betrayed the harsh reality of the attack. It looked like it could have been any other beautiful summer's day, save for the smell of burning metal, which was hot and intense, even from inside the car.

A black orb flew over them, breaking the façade, moving across the remnant of the bridge behind them. Blue light fired again from its core to ensure nothing of it remained.

This is the way the world ends.

Terre swerved between lanes, trying to keep ahead of what he knew would be an inevitable exodus through the outskirts of the city.

"Don't tell me you're going to try to take the 101?" K was hanging onto the door for dear life, struggling not to close his eyes in fear.

"Do you have a better idea?"

"Maybe something that won't be completely gridlocked?"

"That's going to be every road in the city in a few minutes. We need to make as much distance as we can while the road is still clear."

It wasn't going to take long for that to happen. As they passed by downtown, Terre could already tell people were trying to escape the mayhem. Fortunately, at least for the two of them, hardly anyone in San Francisco owned a vehicle.

Terre was an oddity in a city where driverless cars picked people up and dropped them off for a fraction of the cost of owning a vehicle. It also ensured a vehicle was more productive than sitting in a parking space for eighty percent of the day.

Even before bots had started to descend from the void, Terre couldn't stand the thought of being stranded on Treasure Island with no means of transportation. He had bought the old hatchback when he'd arrived in the city. It wasn't hard to find someone ready to get rid of theirs. But he was thankful now that he had made the purchase.

Their good fortune, though, would be short-lived. The entire Financial District would now be trying to call a car at the same time. The streets were going to be absolute bedlam. And for those stuck downtown, it meant they were going to have a hell of a time getting out of the city.

If they could get past the airport, they'd likely be in the clear, although that was being a little optimistic, in Terre's opinion. But be that as it may, he didn't see any other option to break free of the city's core and reach K's office.

Their hope didn't last long. As they turned south along the freeway, a wall of cars appeared in front of them. They lurched to a complete standstill.

"So much for that," K remarked.

They had made it past the Zuckerberg Hospital, which was something, at least, but it wasn't going to be good enough. Every minute they stayed in the city, the risk of their mission failing was growing exponentially.

Terre saw an opportunity and turned off the nearly empty ramp onto Cesar Chavez. With everyone intent on leaving the city as quickly as possible, perhaps they would overlook alternate routes. He drove through industrial backstreets, trying to find a way around the developing traffic jam on the freeway.

K tapped the screen on the center console. "I can't get your navigation app to load. Is it broken?"

"Cell towers are likely jammed," Terre replied. "Everyone's trying to call loved ones, or livestreaming as the city burns."

"Do you know where you're going?"

They were passing industrial shops. Most appeared to be transport companies that had ditched most of their human employees in favor of automated systems. The driverless trucks would come and go according to schedule, not requiring human intervention. Which meant fewer people.

However, increasing congestion forced them to turn onto a side street, which appeared to be much more pedestrian. Terre wasn't even sure what street they were on, but suddenly coffee shops and bars lined the sidewalks.

One of the black orbs flew overhead. More than one drink spilled on the patio as patrons stood up, mouths agape, their eyes to the sky. Many began to move, not sticking around for the attack to reach them, but others seemed frozen in place, as if unsure whether the carnage happening before them was real.

Another burst of blue light flew out of the Onyx's black surface and plunged into the city. It wasn't apparent what the beam had hit, but it was now clear to those who had been seemingly oblivious before that they were indeed under attack. Screams and chaos erupted. People ran into the street, a few dashing for vehicles while others scrambled to unlock bicycles parked on the sidewalk. Others just ran.

The brakes on Terre's vehicle slammed automatically to avoid a cyclist cutting across the street in front of them.

"Watch where you're going!" Terre yelled out after him.

"We're under attack!" the twenty-something hipster yelled back at him. "Aliens are here, and they're *pissed!*"

"Aliens?" Terre repeated to himself. He looked skyward at

the black entity flying overhead. He guessed, to some, it would seem like an alien invasion.

The street soon filled with people pouring out of houses, coffee shops, and stores in search of safety.

"Guess this is the end of the road. Come on!"

Terre unbuckled and opened the car door.

"What are you doing?" K protested. "You can't seriously be thinking about *walking* to Silicon Valley?"

"We're sure as hell not going to be able to drive there. Besides, we only need to make it to the airport."

Chapter Five

Terre and K jogged down the street, doing their best to avoid the growing number of people also trying to flee. Wide-eyed pedestrians frantically called loved ones, while others were crying or yelling into their eye-pieces and phones. A few spoke with a feigned sense of calm, their tones telling loved ones to stay put. Others screamed, telling whoever was on the receiving end to get the hell out of the city, with no filter and no regard for the dozens around them trying to calm themselves.

Others held their phones to the sky, taking selfies with the plume of smoke that rose from the San Francisco harbor. Others narrated videos of the carnage, clearly filming through the thin-wired eyepieces floating in front of one eye and wrapping around a single ear to keep it in place. Clearly some people still dreamed of becoming online sensations, by capturing footage of their peers freaking out about the attack on their beloved city.

If he hadn't been there himself, Terre would have thought he was watching something out of a movie or a ridiculous dream.

Terre surveyed their options. K was frantically trying not to get swept away in the pandemonium on a sidewalk jammed with a wave of other pedestrians. The street had fewer people but would be a wall of cars for the foreseeable future.

The orbs had disappeared for the moment. Rather than just indiscriminately firing upon the city, their targets seemed calculated, as though they knew exactly how to inflict the most havoc with minimal effort. The two bridges being their first point of attack could not be written off as coincidence.

Terre scanned the street. They weren't going to get anywhere by walking; they needed a way to get around the crowd. A pair of e-bikes sat chained to the café's bike rack, giving him an idea. Terre glanced around to ensure their owners weren't present. Confident they had been abandoned, or that their owners had been held up, he got to work. He pulled out a Swiss Army knife from his pocket and pried at the lock which held them in place. Lockpicking had been a trick he had learned while he was growing up; part of a past he wasn't particularly proud of, but one that had given him skills to survive in a pinch.

"We're just stealing bikes now?" K crossed his arms, bracing his stance as he did his best not to be toppled by those pushing past him, the crowd either unaware or uncaring of their heist.

"Trust me," Terre said. "If we don't take them, their owners won't have the chance to miss them."

"Where did you learn to pick a lock?"

"It's classified." He gave K a wink.

K glanced around, uneasy.

"Relax, we're the good guys." Terre flashed K a grin.

K lifted his eyes skyward as one of the black orbs made another sweep of the city. "Some might argue we're the bad guys."

Terre let out a sigh. They weren't directly responsible for the attacks, but their own government had taken K's program and modified them into killing machines. They were working for the same institution that had unleashed these machines and now refused to pull the plug to reign them in. He finished unlatching the second bike and rolled one over to K.

"Please tell me you know how to ride one of these things?"

K shot an annoyed glance his way and proceeded to mount the bike. "Let's just get going."

Terre patted Kristopher on the shoulder. "Come on, K. It's the end of the world. Don't take yourself so seriously."

He hopped onto his own bike and rolled into the street. It had been a while since he had ridden a bike himself and, despite his jab at K, he'd never actually ridden an e-bike before. He was a little unsure of how to kick in the peddle assist, but it had to be straightforward. K zipped past him and weaved around the stationary vehicles blocking the street.

"Try to keep up!" he yelled back to him.

"Asshole."

Terre's hands gripped the handlebars tight, and he pushed his way through the traffic. The weight of the weapon strapped to his back made the process a little more treacherous, the slight shift in weight on the bike leaving him unbalanced.

He hadn't gone far before a car door swung into his path, forcing him to swerve at the last second and brace himself, narrowly missing both the door and the adjacent car.

"Watch what you're doing!" he yelled back to the driver.

The driver yelled something in return, but Terre couldn't make out what it was. Probably cursing him. No time to argue.

K's lead didn't last long. The sea of people had abandoned the civility of adhering to walking only on the sidewalk, dominating the entire street. The crowd pushed in around them with no plan or direction. They continued to move, but constantly needing to avoid those in their path made it impossible to maintain any sort of cadence.

Frustrated, K shouted back to him, "Do you plan to ride these death traps all the way to NASA? At this rate, we'll never make it. We'll be shot to oblivion first."

"If we have to, but I hope we'll find something better at the airport."

"After that helicopter crash? No, thanks. I've changed my mind; I'm happy with the bike."

"I don't mean aircraft. There should be a car rental fleet we can access with our credentials. The highway will hopefully clear the further south we get."

Terre had no way of knowing if that was true or not, but they had to push forward regardless.

K nodded and meandered his way down the road again.

More people had made a break for it, crawling out of and abandoning their vehicles. Terre did his best to crawl steadily forward around the doors frenetically being flung open and the pedestrians with their eyes to the sky instead of being focused on where they were running. Multiple people tripped over their own feet or ran into the side of a vehicle in their haste.

The sidewalks were so full, it reminded Terre of the closing stages of a concert. Every coffee shop and bar on the street must have been completely full prior to the attack, especially considering the time had now reached peak hours on a Saturday. Maybe that meant most of those office towers in the distance were emptier than they would have been during the week. He could only hope.

"Excuse me! Coming through!"

Most stepped out of the way, while others gave them dirty glances. Cell phones were knocked from the hands of those not paying attention and onto the pavement below. Terre wasn't even sorry. Those with eye-pieces were standing as though in a daze. It was clear they were filming, but they seemed to have lost grip on reality, ignorant to the fact that they were standing amid a city on the verge of collapse.

The door of an older model passenger van opened abruptly in front of him. Terre slammed on his brakes, his back wheel lifting off the pavement and the momentum nearly tossing him over the handlebars into the vehicle door. The wheel made contact with the road once again, though, and Terre was able to regain his balance. It only occurred to him then that a helmet might have been useful.

"Watch it!" he yelled to the driver. The man, in his mid-sixties, perhaps early seventies, with long graying hair, sunglasses, and a short-sleeved t-shirt, gave him a blank look. He hadn't even noticed the accident he had almost caused, his eyes glued to the sky.

"Sorry, dude," the man drawled. He raised his sunglasses to afford him a better look at the cyclist who addressed him. He put a hand up to his face to offer shade from the sun, his pupils wide. This guy was baked. "We've got bigger problems. Aliens are attacking!"

"It's not aliens," Terre said surlily, trying to slip through the space between the still ajar door and the Honda Civic next to it. If the situation wasn't so dire, the constant alien comments would have amused him. But people were dying, and Terre was trying to do all he could to stop it.

The smell of weed wafting in from the open vehicle told him he wasn't wrong in his assessment of the guy.

"It's our military," Terre offered, but he immediately regretted the comment. Even that tidbit was confidential. It wasn't like this guy would remember, though.

"That's right, bro!" The man had turned back to look at

him, astonished. "The aliens and our military are working together! Claire! You were right!" he called into his van. "You gotta look at this! Whoa!"

The van itself was an antique, —a turn-of-the-century passenger vehicle. The bright blue exterior was an obvious paint job, and Terre briefly wondered if the vehicle had been modified somehow to make it adhere to highway regulations. It was so hard to purchase gasoline at a consumer level these days that it would have cost this couple a fortune to be driving it down the freeway. The paltry amount of noise coming from the old beast indicated they had indeed fitted it with an electric engine, but the car didn't appear to have any form of autonomous controls built in, and Terre didn't want to fathom what the insurance must have been costing them. Automation meant fewer accidents, and thus lower premiums. It wouldn't be long before a car wouldn't be allowed on the road without it.

Terre glanced into the van to see an elderly woman passed out on the passenger seat, her mouth open, snoring. She'd kick herself later when her boyfriend filled her in on the alien invasion, or she'd roll into the apocalypse blissfully unaware.

Piles of possessions spilled out of the back seat—from groceries to blankets and pillows. It was clear the couple lived in the van. Perhaps they were just on vacation, but Terre guessed this was their retirement; an economical option in a market that wasn't forgiving to the quickly disappearing middle class. Terre rolled his eyes and kept pedaling.

With his path also blocked, it didn't take long for Terre to catch up to K. Once he did, the pair gained some ground. The further they progressed away from downtown, the fewer people there were crowding their path.

Beyond the cafés and bars, residential properties lined the

streets. Most of the populace who had been fleeing moments ago must have lived nearby and sought shelter at home. Victorian style houses, though iconic in San Francisco, seemed out of place in contrast to the surrounding industrial buildings. They stood defiant, imitating the style gentrifying the area.

Onlookers stared out their windows, curious about the commotion. But with no visible line of sight to the bay, there was no urgency to flee. The most they would be able to make out from their living rooms was a slight increase in traffic. The crowd had dwindled to no more than a trickle.

Good. Best place for anyone was going to be indoors. If streets this far from the conflict began flooding with people, things were going to escalate in a hurry. It wouldn't take much for things to go from bad to worse. It was likely lockdowns would start to be enforced soon. If the bots didn't take to firing on the homes first.

The only evidence here that something was amiss was the ever-growing pillar of smoke rising in the distance. How much of the downtown would be left after this?

Until now, adrenaline had fueled both technicians, but the exertion of cycling meant that K quickly needed a rest. Terre pulled up next to K and brought a hand to his forehead to wipe the sweat that was dripping down into his eyes. The scorching July sun was unrepentant.

Terre took off his jacket. He had a decision to make, and he didn't like either option. He reluctantly tossed the coat on the ground, regretting grabbing it in the cool, breezy morning air. The heat of the day and the workout he was getting made the jacket too much to handle, and the Drone Surge on his back had already added an extra layer of bulk, causing the cloying sweat to stick to his back.

That jacket might have been the most expensive piece of clothing Terre owned, but it was best to cut his losses to afford some small sense of relief. He could add his favorite jacket to the list of things these bots had already cost him. The sacrifice was small when compared with the damage faced by the city, and he admonished himself for being selfish over such a trivial item. The losses were getting to him, though, no matter how insignificant.

He fumbled at the top buttons of his button-down shirt to provide himself with a bit more room to breathe. The shirt clung to him, damp from the sweat pouring from him amid the humidity of the afternoon. At least it had short sleeves, but they provided little comfort.

Terre allowed his hand to wrap around the robot medallion around his neck. Andersen had at least been occupied mostly by soldiers and their families; those who had signed up to put themselves in harm's way. Not a single person in the ravaged downtown had likely imagined their own country's military would be virtually powerless to stop autonomous drones from turning on their own city. But however much at fault their government was for letting this continue, Terre and K had the chance to stop it—to prevent more lives from being lost.

"Do we need to get back on the freeway?" K asked, breaking Terre free from his thoughts. The noise on the street had reduced to a mild hum now that vehicles and people had disappeared. It was baffling how the chaos could go from a hundred to zero in a matter of only a few blocks.

"We can follow Bayshore there. It should be less congested and less hazardous than two dupes on the freeway on their bikes."

"It's going to take us at least an hour to get to the airport. Those things will have completely destroyed the city before we have chance to get there."

As if responding to K's concern, two fighter jets roared overhead.

"Hopefully, those two can hold them off for now. My main concern is whether these two rogue orbs are the only ones to hit the city today, or if we can expect their friends to follow."

The jets made another pass overhead, firing both conventional and energy-based projectiles. The shots were lost in the distance, toward the cityscape, their eventual destination invisible from where the two IT specialists stood.

"Two on two. Let's hope they can take them down."

"The Air Force will send more fighters. These are just the first response."

The 101 freeway passed them by, elevated and adjacent to the empty service road they traveled on. Above them, cars were still immobilized, vacated by their passengers. Terre and K stood to the side of the road, hands held high to block out the afternoon sun, as they tried to gain some perspective of the fight that echoed above them and to the north.

Now free of the congestion, they had been making good mileage. Despite the amount he was sweating, Terre wasn't out of breath, even at the pace they maintained. Either his trips to the gym the last six weeks were paying off, or those tiny bots in his bloodstream were doing their job.

His recovery physio was meant to help him regain his strength, but it had also provided Terre with much needed distraction. Some of the PTs had told him he was training too frequently, pushing his body too quickly for his condition. He didn't care. Being on leave and having nothing else to fill his time had enabled his mind to turn dark quickly. He couldn't let himself dwell on the loss of those who had meant the most to him. Dr. Ballast had told him the extra sessions were okay unless he felt fatigued, but Terre had never felt better physically. The nanobots were like a shot of caffeine to the bloodstream.

Perhaps unrealized rage drove him onward, or perhaps

redirected feelings of inadequacy. Terre didn't dwell on the *why*. His workouts had never been more intense; never more satisfying.

The progress was quick. After six weeks, he was stronger, with more stamina than he'd had even in his twenties.

Now was no different. He felt great, though he could do without the sweating. He wondered if the nanos were making him sweat more or less. It made no difference, but for the sake of his own comfort, he hoped they wouldn't have to take the e-bikes past the airport.

Terre patted K on the shoulder, signaling their rest was over, and propelled his bike forward.

Half an hour into their ride, the light traffic their service road held was still flowing freely. Self-driving vehicles still jammed the nearby 101, as if it were rush hour on a Friday afternoon. Terre looked at his watch: twelve-thirty p.m. on a Saturday. Every car in the city must have been trying to make an exit.

The roar of another plane sounded in the distance. Ahead of them, a passenger jet dropped deep into its descent toward the runway. It took Terre a moment for the gravity of the situation to weigh on him. Why was air traffic being allowed to continue? San Francisco airspace was literally gripped in a battle for the city's survival, and a plane full of passengers was descending right into the combat zone.

Those fighter jets would have been dispatched from a base further east. Terre expected SFO Airport to be closed. This had to have been an oversight. They didn't need additional collateral in this whole mess.

"Phone, call Fredricks," he said as he pulled the device from his back pocket. The phone went directly to video, which was a bit cumbersome while on the bike, but Fredricks would have to deal with his shoddy cinematography. In moments like these, Terre had to admit he could see how an eye-piece or even an implant would come in handy, but the idea of being constantly connected to his device didn't sit right with him.

The Technology Supervisor answered almost immediately. "Hoffman, where are you? We're trapped on the island. Still trying to shoot these things down. The jets seem to be more effective, but we've only got ..."

"We're almost at the airport," Terre interrupted. "We were slowed down in the city, but we'll make up for it. Fredricks, why are passenger jets still flying into the area? We've got a 747 over our heads on its way into SFO!"

"The airspace should be closed to all civilian traffic. I'm on it," was his reply, and he hung up.

"What was that about?" K pulled back and asked.

Terre pointed at the jet, still descending as they spoke.

"This should be a no-fly zone! Those bots took out that news helicopter with no regard for ..."

Harsh blue light pierced the sky and an explosion rocked the front of the plane, flipping it end-over-end.

On a course heading straight for them.

Debris flew in every direction. Shards of metal and glass rained down, the plane itself splitting into three mammoth pieces. The cockpit broke apart and plummeted below. Terre couldn't see its final destination, but he hoped it wasn't on top of someone's house.

The body and tail carried on with the momentum, continuing to cartwheel in the air. Smoke and debris followed in its wake. Terre tried not to pay attention to the bodies flying out, keeping his eyes on the road in front of him.

Until the fuselage made contact with the freeway.

The earth shook as metal impacted against concrete, in the horrifying resound of a thunderous roar and nauseating screech that Terre could feel reverberating through his core.

The body of the plane lurched along the open road, ripping up the elevated freeway ahead of them, scattering earth, rocks, vehicles, and anything else that stood in its path. A wing snapped off and continued rolling, embedding itself into the side of an industrial warehouse a couple of blocks away.

A cloud of dust billowed from the point of impact, enveloping them, and blotting out anything else in the wreckage's vicinity.

Unable to see the road in front of them, Terre and K were forced to stop. Flames slowly became visible as they licked at the remains of the crash, hungry for what little was left of the crumpled heap.

Nobody could have survived that.

Dust slowly settled around them. K's stunned expression said it all. Despite everything they had already seen, the descent of the passenger jet was nearly impossible to comprehend. Despite having tried to avoid looking, Terre couldn't quite shake the image of passengers, still strapped to their seats, falling from the sky as their plane somersaulted into even more unsuspecting civilians below.

The military jets roared above them as they performed a wide arc, surveying the wreck. Blue beams fired toward them, but with maneuverability the pilot of a commercial plane could never even dream of, they managed to dodge the laser fire at the last second. A hillside behind them erupted in flames as the evaded discharge made contact.

They needed to get this program installed before more AI units were unleashed; before the bots killed any more people.

Sirens rang from the direction of the airport. Firetrucks and ambulance crews would be on their way, but they'd have a tough time getting close to the wreckage with the collapsed freeway and surrounding roads being torn up for miles. Visibility around them had improved, but dust still hung thick in the air. Dark roiling smoke was soon to replace anything the dust hadn't overtaken. It appeared they'd be mostly riding blind the rest of the way.

Another explosion in the distance shook the ground beneath their feet, its epicenter in the direction of downtown. Hopefully, it was a bot being taken down and not another building collapsing. The jets ascended and began circling at a higher altitude before departing the area.

They must have neutralized the situation.

For now.

"Let's keep going." Terre motioned to K. "Things aren't going to get any better until we fix this mess."

Chapter Six

"I'm sorry, sir. I need to see some ID."

The security guard at San Francisco International Airport was being a pain. The man, in his early twenties, stood fast before them, his light blue eyes eager, betraying him to be fresh on the job. Robots, explosions, fighter jets; this kid was either thrilled at the excitement or terrified. Some of these fresh hires let the uniform and the gun get to their heads. This guy didn't rub Terre that way, on account of there being no condescension in the guard's tone.

His blond hair had been shaved back, but his face still possessed a layer of baby fat that betrayed any sense of authority. A few more months of airport meals and a slowing metabolism would likely ensure the kid grew into his loose-fitting uniform.

The guard was practically shaking, his eyes darting more than once to the weapons hanging from Terre's belt and slung over his back. Their passes had at least provided them the ability to carry arms through the airport.

Maybe it was more than just the robots making the guard nervous. Either way, the kid was likely afraid he would screw this up.

"Look, I've got my CIA ID," Terre continued, "and security clearance documentation. Look at this. CIA Priority Clearance. What more do you need?"

"Sir, we are on a Critical Threat Level Zero. There has been an attack on US soil. Nobody comes in or out without proper credentials. This says you're an IT staffer, and your friend here works for NASA. You might have clearance during standard operations, but not today. Now, please, I have lots to do."

"Look, can you call whoever it is you need to call and confirm our clearance? We've got a chopper waiting for us at the end of Terminal One."

"What is your involvement in this incident, sir?"

"That's classified." Terre uncrossed his arms and put his hand to his temple. "Look, one simple call, and this will all be cleared up."

The guard took another hard look at the documents in his hand and shook his head.

"Wait right here. I'll go make a call. Have a seat."

The guard disappeared into a back room. K sat down, nervously running his hands through his hair. Blue plastic chairs lined the wall beneath windows overlooking the tarmac. Uniformed men and women jogged toward military aircraft, then they turned and continued running. They weren't boarding; they were running laps. On standby, Terre guessed.

The rest of the airport had been a nightmare to navigate, with passengers frantic to cancel flights after witnessing another plane being shot from the sky. Others panicked, trying to ascertain if their loved ones had been aboard the downed craft. Still others were irate that flights were being canceled at all. One downed plane apparently wasn't enough to convince them their schedules should be interrupted.

The FAA had completely locked the airport down, as well as the country. The crash on the freeway had ensured that all American commercial and private flights had been grounded, and the airports were locked down to secure any threats.

Those within the terminal didn't quite understand that even if they were to be let out, there would be nowhere for them to go. The roads in and out of the airport were completely gridlocked.

Terre and K had gotten through with their credentials. It had been surprisingly easy. Airport security had bigger issues to deal with than two tech nerds trying to get *into* the airport, despite obviously being armed. Then, after navigating the pandemonium of the terminals, the tired and angry stuck on a layover, wondering if they would ever see their loved ones again, the two technicians hit their first roadblock, in the form of this young security guard at the military's private gate.

The door behind them opened and closed again. The same guard came out, still looking at the yellow piece of paper in his hand.

"Sir, I don't have authority to let you through at this time."

"Give me a break, kid. Who's your supervisor?"

"Sir?"

"Never mind." Terre pulled his phone out from his back pocket. "Phone, call Fredricks."

The call was answered before it even rang.

"Hoffman!" Fredricks barked. His face was looking more ragged and worn than it had even an hour earlier. "Where the hell are you? The chopper's been waiting on you for twenty minutes. Get your ass over there!"

"We're trying, sir. We're being held up by a rookie at the gate."

"'Being held up?'"

"The security guard here is doing his best, sir, but he's refusing to let us through."

"You have *got* to be shitting me. I'll send someone to get you."

"Thank you, sir."

The phone clicked off. Terre gave a smile and a nod to K, who didn't notice, and a two-fingered salute to the guard, who pretended not to.

Kristopher sat in a chair in front of one of the bay windows, his vacant eyes staring at the floor. Behind him, planes sat in stasis. There was no way to tell whether there were still passengers on board, but from the rumors he had overheard while navigating the terminals, more than one plane hadn't let people off yet.

"K? What's up, buddy?"

"What?" K asked as Terre's voice jolted him from his stupor. "Oh, nothing. Just thinking about that downed plane. Thinking about the bridge collapsing and everyone crashing into the bay. All because of a system I designed. If we can't stop it …" He shook his head, his hand scratching the edge of his eyebrows. "How can I keep going knowing that?"

"This is not your fault, K," Terre replied. "Get your head in the game. I know we're not used to seeing this type of action, but we've got to stay focused until we get your program uploaded."

"Yeah, I know."

Terre sat down next to K and put a hand on his shoulder. "We've got the means to shut these things down. We're going to save lives."

K looked him dead in the eye. "That doesn't help those lives we've already lost. These are machines I helped design. Machines I helped program."

"You didn't program them to *kill*. Your program is helping to build the Mars colony. What someone else did to your schematics, that's not on you."

K looked back at the floor, but he nodded. "I'll feel better once we shut them all down."

The door to the tarmac opened, and a uniformed woman walked through. She definitely had the confidence of a military officer, and her young features were well-defined to the point of striking. Terre tried not to stare.

She walked up to the guard. "Is there a problem here, Charlie?"

"No, ma'am. I was given orders not to let anyone through without appropriate clearance. These two have standard clearance documents, but they're civilians and we're operating under a Level Zero Alert."

"Thank you for your diligence, Private, but these two are critical personnel in this crisis."

She dismissed Charlie and turned to them. Terre didn't even get a chance to gloat. "Kristopher? Terre?"

They stood up. K saluted, and Terre answered with a simple, "Yes, ma'am."

"Please, call me Ali." She extended a hand to greet K first, smiling. "You're civilians. There's no rank between us."

K grabbed her hand with a goofy grin. She exchanged a quick look with him and returned the smile, though hers was smoother than K's.

Her eyes lingered momentarily on him, but it was long enough for Terre to catch it.

"We're happy to help." Terre extended his hand and returned her greeting. "We're still Defense Department staff, so, technically, we will still answer to you."

Her look toward him was a touch more formal and brief.

She shook her head. "I'm just here to take you to the NASA office. We've commandeered a limo to take us to the helipad. It'll be a simple up and down between here and Mountain View. Would normally just send an Uber to take you all the way, but ... well, nobody's going to be driving anywhere for a while."

"What kind of damage are we looking at?" K asked. "Things looked pretty grim on our way out of the city."

Ali shook her head. "I don't think you need me to tell you

it doesn't look good. Downtown's ravaged. Don't expect the skyline to ever look like it once did."

"They're under control, though?" Terre asked. "Or are we still under attack?" Images of both the downed news helicopter and the passenger jet were still fresh in his mind, and his stomach lurched at the thought of flying.

"Everyone's on standby for the moment. We don't know what these damned things are up to. The best we can do is not to be surprised again."

Terre wondered how much of the city was left. The damage those two orbs had done in the ten minutes it had taken Terre and K to cross the bridge would cripple the city for years, never mind the hour it had taken for the jets to take them down.

Now that the freeway heading south had also been demolished by the crashed aircraft, it hit him that the city was completely isolated from the rest of the world. There were other, smaller roads that would bring them south, but none of them were equipped to handle the volume of traffic that was needed to keep goods, services, and people flowing in and out of the city.

"Come on," Ali said. "We need to get going."

She walked them through the exit and into a long, empty corridor. The hallway led around the center they had been sitting in, back toward the main terminal. Signs indicated that they were walking toward the gates at Entrance B.

Ali opened another door, and the warm July sun streamed into the hallway. A black luxury sedan was parked just outside.

"I thought we were flying out of here?"

"We've got to drive to the Coast Guard terminal. That's where the helipad is."

Ali opened the door to the driver's seat. K took the passenger seat, leaving Terre at the back.

"The car's not self-driving?" Terre asked.

"All automated systems in military units have been deactivated, and we're under strict orders to utilize manually operated equipment for the time being, at least. It makes a number of things extremely difficult, but if our drones have been compromised, who knows what else might be at risk?" She glanced back at him. "Better to be safe than sorry."

The ride to the helipad was relatively short and quiet, or at least it was for Terre in the back seat. Ali and K were engrossed in their own conversation about the car's electronics systems, or something to that effect.

Though the vehicle might not have been automated, it didn't mean the specs were any less flashy than those an A-list celebrity would have requested. With the vehicle's fully leather interior, tinted windows, touch-screen panels, and built-in mini-bar, Terre imagined that was exactly what this vehicle was typically used for. He knew there were several superstars who refused to use driverless vehicles.

After an afternoon of cycling in the summer sun, Terre felt a little out of place. He could have used a change of clothes; his dress shirt and suit pants felt grimy and slick against the freshly polished car seat.

Terre's focus drifted from the garish furnishings to the billow of smoke coming from the direction of downtown San Francisco.

The drone attack might have been halted, but the fight was not over. How many lives had been lost today? All because some military-funded program had decided to turn tech built for space colonization into war machines.

Command could end this now. All it would take was a targeted EMP on the storage facilities housing the Sentinels, Onyx, and other associated designs. But someone had made the decision that the risk of human casualties didn't supersede the trillions of dollars invested.

Terre held onto the medallion around his neck as they drove up to the landing pad.

"The President has just ordered all non-essential air travel be grounded." Ali hit the command panel as she hung up the phone.

"You were on the phone with the President?" Terre yelled over the noise of the chopper blades. The helicopter was on its descent over the Mountain View cityscape. The flight had only been in the air for a few minutes.

"Don't be a dipshit. That was my commanding officer!" she yelled back.

"Just trying to lighten the mood."

"Yeah, well, don't! We've lost a lot of civilian life tonight. People are rioting in the streets of every major city in the country, afraid they might be next. The Pentagon has ordered all major American cities into lockdown, and they're sending troops into the streets."

"I didn't know."

"Let's just get you to your little space computer. I don't know why I was put in charge of you today, but this better be worth my time."

K brought a hand to her shoulder and nodded. "It is! We've got a plan to bring all this to an end."

She softened but still gave him a look of skepticism. "Yeah, well, you better hope it works!"

The view from the air highlighted the damage the assault had caused. Smoke billowed from the ruined downtown. The bots had completely leveled most of the skyscrapers, and those that still stood bore gaping wounds filled with flame and devastation.

The freeways were gridlocked from the peninsula all the

way down the bay and the coastline until they faded in the distance. It would have taken them hours to have traveled down to Mountain View on their e-bikes, and only if they had managed to circumnavigate the hysteria that was gripping the streets.

It was hard to tell from the air exactly what was happening below, but Terre could make out a fair number of red and blue lights. Army vehicles and soldiers marched through the streets, the National Guard having been called into force, protecting what remained from looting and ensuring those injured or affected by the attack had somewhere safe to go.

The flight was unsurprisingly short, only a few minutes for them to reach the southern tip of the Bay. As they descended into Mountain View, Terre could make out Levi's Stadium, only a few miles away in nearby Santa Clara, and dozens of FEMA personnel already making preparations, setting up beds, tents, and supplies to aid those who had just been displaced.

Below them, newly developed office towers stood delicately beside the waterfront. K's office was situated within a private enterprise complex, and not within the actual NASA research center. There was no place for his software development program amongst the development of highly specialized equipment. During their time on base, K had explained to Terre that his office's location had made his commute a little less arduous and a little more relaxed. Instead, he sat next to those who developed artificial intelligence for the consumer market. His peers developed tech toys for industry, but it had kept him fresh with the latest trends and advancements.

As their chopper touched down on the roof of a central tower, a fireball streaked several yards above them and slammed into a nearby building. Terre would have fallen out of his seat if he hadn't been strapped in, and K noticeably jumped. Warmth from the missile's explosion reached the interior of the cabin as the affected structure erupted into flames.

Ali cursed, but the whir of the engine muffled it. She unbuckled herself and jumped into the cockpit to speak to the pilot.

With the blades powered down and the engine killed, their pilot, a serviceman named Gary Rupert, stepped out of the cockpit, pushing his way past Ali. A ball of muscle, Gary made no qualms about getting off the aircraft and into the building as quickly as possible. He adjusted his sunglasses from the bridge of his nose to atop his cropped-short hair. The man was middle-aged, clean-shaven, and clearly not in the mood for nonsense—exactly what Terre expected from a helicopter pilot.

"Let's go!" Gary said. "We've got to get indoors!"

"You're coming with us?" K asked.

"Were you not paying attention? A drone just shot a missile over our heads. That building is on fire. I'm not sitting on this roof a minute longer than I have to, and I'm sure as hell not flying again." He pointed to a building several blocks away that had suffered the brunt of the missile that had been meant for them.

Smoke billowed into the sky as wailing sirens echoed above the noise of the street below. Fighter jets had been quick to respond this time around. The sound of aerial combat raged overhead.

"What now?" Terre managed, unbuckling his seatbelt and stumbling over himself as he tried to stand up. Even just the short flight in the chopper had made him unsteady on his feet.

"More drones," K answered.

Terre instinctively looked to the sky as two triangle-shaped planes flew overhead. These were the standard Predator drones he was used to seeing while on base, similar to those that had attacked Guam six weeks ago. He unconsciously grabbed the robot pendant around his neck. Memories of Cara pushed through, and he didn't want to let her down. Especially now that they were so close to their destination.

"Let's move!" Gary was holding a door open on the other side of the roof.

Terre hazarded a glance behind him to witness Ali giving K a pat on the back. They were hanging back, smiling at each other. This was not the time.

The glow in K's eye disappeared as it met Terre's glare. He hadn't even realized he was scowling until he saw K's face deflate. He tried to wipe the scorn from his face, but he had no way to tell if he was successful or not. The harder he tried, the more ridiculous and tense it felt.

There was no time for this. If K wanted to flirt, it was no concern of his, but they were on a mission. Nothing could interfere with what they came here to do. Plus, with the world crumbling around them, it hardly set the mood for a romantic encounter.

Stress makes the heart cling to ridiculous notions, Terre reminded himself. Maybe there would be time for K and Ali to swoon over each other after they got the updates from K's office.

Terre continued down the stairs, leaving them to catch up. Gary stayed until the door was shut, which meant Terre was taking point down the stairs. The problem was, he had no idea where they were going.

The foundations shook beneath their feet. He raced down the stairs with no other direction to follow. Each of the doors they passed was as gray and non-descript as the last. He assumed that if he needed to exit through one of them, someone would yell at him.

His companions were quiet. K was trying to catch his breath as they vaulted down each set of stairs. The only other sound in the stairwell was that of boots ringing out on the metal steps.

Terre stopped as he reached the ground floor. The building shook again, and he basically fell through the door as he turned the knob.

They spilled out into an open room. Sleek gray tile greeted them. The peak of modern Silicon Valley contemporary style stood in juxtaposition to the dark cement and metal of the stairway. Large windows allowed an enhanced view of those walking by.

"The drones must have moved on." Ali approached the window. She allowed her gaze to wander across the sky.

Terre risked a glance out the window, skyward. The drones that had been targeting their helicopter were nowhere to be seen.

"The drones seem at their most aggressive against aerial activity," Terre thought out loud.

"What are you talking about?" K asked.

"The news helicopter; the passenger jet; us. They're claiming the airspace as their own."

K lifted a skeptical eye.

"Think about it. We're nowhere near the epicenter of the attack, and yet we narrowly missed being shot down. We land, and the drones move on. I don't think there's a coincidence."

"You might be on to something," Ali said. "I'll radio that theory in. It's worth considering." She turned her attention to K. "All right, computer guy. Where are we headed?"

Kristopher was also looking out the window, oblivious to the question.

"Where's your office, K?"

The sound of metal and glass colliding shook the building. A fireball crashed into the street beside them. The road lit up, as cars, trees, and whatever else was incinerated by a giant wall of flame.

So much for my theory.

An SUV plowed through a wall, hit a piece of debris, flipped over, and skidded into the side of a mail truck. A uniformed man jumped out of the vehicle, now laying on its side. He hurled himself toward the side of the road as his truck burst into flames.

"We've got to stop this!" Terre said, his voice firm. "We need to get that program uploaded! *Now!*"

"I've got to grab a clearance key. Hang on, I'll be right back." K sprinted toward the front desk.

The SUV was resting on its wheels, but its side had been embedded into the underbelly of the mail truck. Terre could see the shadow of a lifeless woman pressed against the steering wheel.

Movement in the back seat caught his eye. Someone was back there.

A kid.

A little girl.

Her brown hair was caught on something, and she was banging on the window.

In a flash, the girl was Sarah, her big brown eyes staring through their living room window in Guam. She pressed her hands against the glass, crying out for her daddy to save her.

The house they had rented in Guam had been a quaint little bungalow, with two bedrooms and a small living space that had included a kitchen and living room. Sarah would often have stood at the window, her face pressed against the glass, waiting for Terre to come home at the end of a long shift.

When proximity detectors and sensors weren't malfunctioning, Terre was fortunate in the hours he kept. The late nights were few, and the stress in his position had been fairly low. But every evening around dinnertime, Sarah would wait at the window, her small breath fogging an area around her face.

His nightmares had plagued him during the weeks following the attack. In his dreams, Sarah was rooted to her usual spot, waiting for him to return. She stood there, smiling. Sometimes he could see her mouthing the words "Daddy" or "help" before there was a sudden flash and the house was obliterated. Sometimes the dreams were more graphic; a mangled body asking why he didn't help them; why he didn't come for her and her mom. But he pushed those nightmares down deep and didn't allow himself to explore the reality of what might or might not have happened that day.

But now he had another chance.

Flames erupted, teasing the edges of the vehicle. Giant blocks of cement and metal beams zig-zagged across the street and sidewalk around them.

"Sarah!" he yelled. He pushed his way out the door and sprinted into the street.

"Terre! Stop!" He heard Ali call from somewhere behind him. But he had to rescue his little girl. He wasn't going to fail her again.

Sweat dripped down his face and back as the heat of the inferno boiled around him. Aside from the mail truck, a nearby food truck and coffee stand had also caught on fire. Tiny hands banged against the glass of the SUV. The kid inside was desperate to break the shatterproof glass.

In an instant, Terre was there, his hand reaching through the window he had shattered with his bare hands. He didn't remember deciding to break the glass—it was just suddenly gone—and he worked to clear glass out of the way.

Before he could clear enough debris to climb inside, a metal post creaked next to them. A cringe-inducing shriek filled the air as it came toppling down. Terre barely had enough time to jump out of the way before it crashed onto the hood of the SUV, shaking its frame and pulling the vehicle upward. The front of the cabin crumpled under the force. The impact covered the mom's lifeless body inside, before the car rolled onto its side. The girl's scream filled the air as the momentum of the vehicle tossed her about.

Once the post stopped bouncing on the car's surface, Terre rushed back to the vehicle's side.

"It's okay, it's okay," he said as he opened the back hatch of the vehicle.

Nothing is okay, said a voice in his head. *Nothing about this is okay. But I won't let you die, like I did my family. I won't. I won't let those damn bots take you, too.*

"Are you hurt?" he managed.

Tears streamed down the girl's face. She was scared. Terrified.

The back wheels of the vehicle spun in midair, as desperate as the girl to escape, the crushed well jamming its front wheels. The automation system should have shut off after an accident, but in its destroyed state, it was instead telling the vehicle to accelerate.

Terre fought desperately with the door handle of the back hatch, but because the vehicle thought it was currently cruising down the freeway at eighty miles per hour, the system had the door locked tight.

The only way to get to the girl was going to be through the window. Terre didn't hesitate. He removed the CD-52 that was slung over his back and leaned it against the SUV. He pushed himself through the space where the shattered pane once was, ignoring cuts and scrapes as small fragments brushed past his arms—he had nothing to remove them with and no time to do so. He shuffled his lumbering frame over the seating, doing his best to further avoid the metal and glass that littered the interior. Smoke filling the cab threatened to choke him, and the girl coughed as it filled her lungs. Scrapes and bruises marred her arms and face, but from what Terre could tell, the girl looked as though she had weathered the assault, mostly unharmed. At least physically. Who knew what sort of mental trauma the girl would face in the years to come.

She shook uncontrollably. Tears filled her eyes, and her little hands went to her face to cover the horror no young child should ever have to witness.

Glass from the building across the street continued to fall onto the exterior of the SUV. The patter of falling pieces sounded like hail raining against its surface. Larger pieces shook the vehicle as they struck the bodywork. Terre winced at each vibration, fearing the windows above them would shatter—or another large piece of debris would land on the vehicle, crushing them both.

Even more frightening was the prospect that the flames circling the vehicle's edges would breach the battery and ignite the lithium within—it was a matter of when, not if. If it happened before they could escape the vehicle, they would both be cooked alive.

Instead of crawling closer to him, the girl had curled up in a ball. With the car still on its side, her feet rested on top of the mangled door, glass from its window crunching beneath her feet. With fire raging all around, Terre needed to convince her to comply, and quickly.

"It's okay," he soothed. "I'm here to help. What's your name?"

The girl sniffed a few times and wiped her face on the sleeve of her pink jacket. "Krystal," she said hesitantly.

"Okay, Krystal. I'm here to help you, but I need your help, too, okay? I'm going to get you someplace safe."

"Is my mom going to be okay?"

Terre froze.

Chapter Seven

Cara kissed him goodbye at the doorstep. He'd had to turn off that damn alarm. The alarm that had been warning them something was wrong for two damn weeks before the drones had descended.

The drones had obliterated the residences where Terre and his wife and daughter had spent the last two years. How had he not acknowledged that the alarm was a symptom of a bigger problem?

If only he had known. If he could go back, kiss his wife, hold his daughter close, he would have held on longer. As long as he could.

Cara's face stared at him from behind their living room window as it had imploded in the shockwave, moments before the warhead made impact and left their home a hole in the ground.

He hadn't really seen it. Thank God he hadn't been able to see it. But he dreamt it. He saw it every night in the nightmares that kept him from getting a proper night's rest. In some ways, it was worse than reality, because his imagination played games with his head, and it was likely his thoughts were far more graphic.

He had woken up that evening on a flight back to San Francisco, heading for a hospital where he would be injected with those damn nanos. For his survival. One of only a handful of injured worth trying to save.

He'd heard the news on the way over. In fact, he'd asked. He'd asked about his wife. They had to let her know. Let her know he was okay.

They had to send her to meet them, he'd said. He wouldn't leave her and Sarah alone in Guam. They'd want to be with him.

That's when they'd told him. Told him his family hadn't made it. Nobody in the staff residences had made it. Not his family. Not his friends. If he hadn't gone into work so damn early, he wouldn't have made it, either. Not another damn civilian on base except for the kid. And K had only survived because he had been with him in the Command Center.

Most of those on duty hadn't survived, either. They had been caught so unprepared that it was a miracle they had stopped the attack at all. Over eighty percent of the base were killed. Their operations center would be rendered useless for months, probably years, as they tried to rebuild. The United States' largest Pacific military operation off the mainland had been rendered impotent. The U.S. Naval Base, Andersen Air Force Base, and the Marine Corps Base had all been decimated.

Thankfully, not much civilian territory off base had been affected by the attacks. The damage seemed coordinated; strategic. Analysts only confirmed later that the drones had been completely automated and acting with no human guidance.

K had been on the plane as well. The kid had been unconscious, knocked out by falling debris while helping to pull him out of the rubble. Being unconscious would have been a welcome escape, rather than to awaken in this nightmare.

They'd given him the first treatment once he landed. His wounds had been treated and he'd been injected with the nanobots, but there was nothing they could do to heal what the drones had taken from him.

So, he'd pushed it down.

Three weeks after the attack, they'd held the funeral for those not in combat; the families and staff. The fallen troops had had their own state funeral the day before. He had only known them in passing. The President was there; the same President who had funded an accelerated AI program to keep up with the Chinese. The head of the administration who'd authorized the removal of all safety protocols, despite the pleas of the roboticists themselves. Despite the pleas of the head of the technology department who warned that, without any limits, either they or the Chinese would open Pandora's Box.

And, of course, they had, just as they'd predicted. Now, his wife was in the grave, along with three thousand others. Three thousand from the Guam attack alone.

A classified attack.

Almost nobody who hadn't been on the island knew the truth. Nobody would know what was coming for them.

The MPs hadn't wanted to let him back to survey his own house, but he had insisted. He had to see what he could recover. He had to see what had happened to his home.

There had been nothing left except a hole in the ground. He had sifted through the rubble—piles of shattered wooden beams and ash. Nothing. Not even a memento of his family that he could put on a shelf.

The nanobots had begun healing him by then. He'd had two more injections to go, but he'd forced himself to walk despite the pain, despite his legs threatening to buckle beneath him. He forced himself to lift pieces of two-by-four and plywood, burnt to a crisp, hoping to find, at least, a memory buried underneath.

His wife and daughter's remains had been removed. He'd been told ahead of time so that he hadn't been anxious about accidentally coming across their bodies.

He'd found that robot medallion, the one he would later hang over his rearview mirror, and nothing else.

After hours of searching, he couldn't force his legs to keep him upright any longer, and he'd simply let himself fall into the wreckage, until someone came to look for him and carried him back to base.

The wide-eyed girl climbed over the seat in front of her, toward the back of the SUV. Somehow, she had got her dark brown hair loose from whatever it had been tangled in moments before, and she climbed into the arms of the stranger who claimed he would save her.

Terre held his arms out and wrapped them around her, protecting her as he rolled back out of the vehicle and ensured his feet found stable footing. Despite the hotter-than-normal ninety-two-degrees afternoon, Krystal was wearing a pink spring jacket. Her hair had been parted into two braids, each tied off with a matching pink bow.

He picked up the Drone Surge from beside the car where he'd left it, considering if it would be worthwhile to use it, but with his inexperience with weaponry and its limited range, he imagined it would do little good against the drones zipping high in the sky.

Ali had stepped out of the building. Terre had been oblivious to her screams, telling him to ignore the little girl in distress.

"Don't worry, Sarah. I've got you."

"Krystal!" the girl corrected. "Please make sure my mom's okay."

"Someone will check on your mom," he lied. Terre looked over his shoulder at the collapsed cab of the white SUV—the vehicle was completely mangled. It was a miracle Krystal had made it out in one piece. He couldn't bring himself to tell the poor child that her mother was dead.

"Get in here!" Ali was marching toward him, radio in hand.

The street had been all but vacated, except for a few people trying to catch everything on video.

"Everyone, get off the street! It's not safe! Find cover!" Ali yelled at the few remaining onlookers in earshot.

A few moved on.

"Terre, I did not just fly you over here so you could get yourself killed! Get your scrawny ass in here!"

Scrawny?

Another round of drones circled above them. Several fighter jets flew further ahead, trying to gain a position. Trying to avoid more collateral damage. A losing battle.

With Krystal in his arms, he could do nothing but watch as a glass window ten stories above Ali shattered, and a five-foot windowpane came loose from its frame and plummeted. He watched it drop in slow motion.

Terre cried out for her to move.

But there wasn't enough time, not enough context for her to clue into what was happening. Instead, Ali looked up. The horror he had avoided in Guam came to life on the streets of Silicon Valley. The large pane of glass fell square on her forehead.

He cowered away as it sliced into her, shielding Krystal's eyes from witnessing the impact, only the sound of shattering glass on the pavement an indication of the harsh reality of what had just unfolded. For several long moments afterward, he stood there, huddled over Krystal, breathing hard.

"Ali!" Terre could hear K's scream beyond the threshold of the door as the drones circled above, their fight focused elsewhere. More shrapnel dropped around them. He had to get Krystal off the street.

Terre raced back into the office tower. He did his best to avoid Ali's remains, all the while averting both his eyes and Krystal's. But he had to step over the stream of blood that trickled down the sidewalk. He felt sick. Absolutely sick. He'd raced out to save one life and lost another. Another person dead because of him.

Krystal's feeble whimpers vibrated against his chest. She likely couldn't see anything that had happened around them, but the yelling, the explosions, and the crying from up and down the street couldn't have been anything but traumatizing.

Those who had earlier been indifferent to the destruction had seemingly vanished. The few who remained were determinedly seeking refuge or aiding those who had been injured.

It suddenly dawned on him that he didn't know where to take her. He had saved Krystal from the fiery crash and had promised her protection, but in reality, he had none to give.

The earth shook violently beneath his feet, and heat radiated against Terre's backside. He only cast enough of a glance over his shoulder to catch what remained of the white SUV bursting into a ball of flame. The battery had been breached, and within seconds, the vehicle had become the charred metal cage he had feared.

Terre turned back to the office tower and pulled the back of Krystal's pink jacket up and over her head to ensure she still couldn't see either the remnants of her family's former vehicle or Ali's body on the sidewalk as they walked through the door.

"What the hell?" K was clawing at his face as if he was about to tear his skin off, his gaze fixed on Ali lying dead on the sidewalk.

"We can't deal with her now," said Terre.

"'We can't *deal* with her now?' What are you talking about? We can't just leave her there! We have to do something!" The kid was hyperventilating. He grabbed the doorway with both hands, his knuckles white, his face turning green as if he were about to vomit.

"K, listen to me." Terre gripped K's shoulder tightly with one arm while trying to maintain his grip on Krystal with the other. He forced K to make eye contact with him. "She's dead. I can't think about it right now."

Can't think about it because it's my fault. She's dead because of me. I don't want anyone else to die because of me. Not Krystal. Not anyone. We need to keep moving.

Terre choked back how he really felt. He knew he wasn't properly processing what was happening. But there was a girl he was clinging to who hadn't been burned alive because of him. That was worth something, wasn't it?

A life for a life. Just not his own.

But there was no time for self-condemnation; no time to mourn. They had to put a stop to the killing.

"There's nothing we can do for her." Terre could feel the coldness in his voice. "And we have to get this done. We need to get that program uploaded."

K's eyes focused on Terre's as he gained control of his breathing. Terre hoped he'd be able to hang in there a little longer. He hoped they both could.

"Who's the girl?" K asked after a moment, his eyes downcast, avoiding meeting Terre's gaze.

"Someone who needed help." Terre exhaled a sigh of relief. He had expected a deeper confrontation. K had quickly attached himself to Ali, and Terre expected the blame for her death to be fully placed on his shoulders. Terre could take K hating him—he hated himself. But whatever penance he'd be forced to pay would have to wait. "Is there anyone around here we can leave her with?"

He took a deep breath, as he felt his own hold on things slipping away from him.

How many dead people was this going to take?

Chapter Eight

"Will my mom be here soon?" Krystal looked at Terre, her eyes moist with both hope and fear.

"We'll find out," K answered, firing a scowl at Terre as he gave a slight shake of his head. He took the girl's hand and led her into the lobby.

K was angry at him, and he deserved it. Terre had saved the girl's life, but at what cost? Ali was dead because of it. But what was he supposed to have done?

An elderly woman was cowering behind a reception desk in the center of the large foyer that stretched out between them. Glasses, which normally hung from her neck on a chain, were perched on the bridge of her nose as she stood looking wide-eyed out the window. She shook uncontrollably, ignoring the ringing phone as she watched the flames illuminating the street outside.

"Alice, could you take this girl to the daycare?" K asked her as he approached the desk. "And then please call the police."

Alice's eyes didn't leave the street. Her lip quivered. She wordlessly pointed to the door as two officers walked in. Both looked as shell-shocked as the rest of them.

One was a stocky man with a mustache, chewing gum as if he had just been auditioning for a bad cop show. The other was a red-headed kid who couldn't have spent much time in uniform. He looked around nervously, as if expecting someone to blow his cover and reveal to the world that his first week on the job happened to coincide with the end of the world.

"Excuse me," the stocky officer blurted out mid-chew. "We realize you're likely aware of this, but we're currently under attack."

Alice just nodded. K stood looking at them blankly.

Terre let out a short laugh, even though it wasn't funny. He couldn't help but see the irony in the midst of the world crumbling around them. "Is that what that was?"

The stocky one—D. Arnold, according to the name tag on his chest—continued, as if Terre had said nothing. "The entire state is currently in lockdown. Nobody, other than emergency personnel, are to venture outside, for any reason. We realize this is a scary situation. This is not an invasion. We are being advised that some of our country's military equipment has malfunctioned. If there is a basement to this building, we ask that you go there for your own protection."

Alice continued to nod and wordlessly reached under her desk to grab a small handbag. She held it up in front of her as if it would protect her from the next blast. As if on cue, the building shook slightly, as something outside either exploded or fell.

"Sir, we have this little girl. Her mom was in that SUV outside." Terre pointed to the flaming wreckage in the street, mostly hidden by a black ball of smoke. "The woman didn't make it. And neither did one of our colleagues. Part of the building fell on her. She's still lying outside."

Arnold put his hands in the air. "We'll make a note the girl's here, but there's a lot of kids who are going to be without parents after today. Sorry, buddy; there's nothing else we can do right now. Roadways are jammed. We're going door-to-door on foot, telling people to stay inside and take cover. The National Guard has been deployed, but as you can imagine, there's more going on than our resources can manage. She doesn't look like she's injured, so take her to the basement for now. We'll move your friend off the sidewalk, but that's all we can do until more help arrives."

K gave Terre another nasty look. His black mop of hair had fallen flat with sweat.

"Is someone going to help my mom?" Krystal cried.

"We're working on it, kiddo." K was already losing patience at having a child in tow. "Alice, can you please take Krystal down to the basement? Let the daycare workers know she's with me and to keep the children down there occupied. Try not to scare them, but also let them know nobody can come upstairs for now. We'll get someone else to inform the rest of the building."

Alice looked down at the sticky child that had found her way into their lives. Terre reluctantly let go of her hand as Krystal looked up at the woman with graying curly hair and a bewildered look.

"Are you a gramma?" the girl asked her, wiping a fresh batch of snot on her pink sleeve.

The girl's presence awakened Alice, and she let out a big, genuine smile. This lady was definitely a 'gramma.'

"As a matter of fact, I am. And you must be a princess?"

"Noo!" An enormous grin lit the child's face. It was as if the world hadn't just crumbled around her. Terre's heart sank as he pondered what her future held. At least she was still here. It was because of him she was still here.

He tried to reassure himself he had done the right thing. He had saved a young life. The curly brown locks that bobbed down the hall toward the stairwell gave credence to that fact. But it was also because of him that Ali wasn't, and he wasn't sure if he was going to be able to let that go.

"Well, my mistake. With that pretty pink jacket, you look

just like a princess! Do you want to go downstairs? I bet there are toys down there."

The girl nodded emphatically and reached for Alice's hand. "My gramma always has candy in her purse."

"Well, let's go downstairs and I'll see what I can find for you." She gave K a sweet smile.

Krystal chattered Alice's ear off down the hall to the flight of stairs, and she disappeared with her newfound 'gramma' to the basement.

"What the hell was that?" K said, grabbing the collar of Terre's shirt and pushing him against the wall.

Terre winced, anticipating a fist to his jaw, but instead he was able to push K off with little effort. Instead of winding up for a punch, the shaggy-haired technician just stood there, panting, his fists clenched. He appeared to be debating with himself—possibly calculating the odds of how effective an attack might be.

Terre stood his ground and readied his stance in case K came barreling at him, but tried to appear non-threatening, breathing as calmly as he could manage. His adrenaline had spiked, but he refused to make the next move. He could feel his pulse in his chest; blood pumping through his veins, preparing his body for the fight or flight that was potentially coming.

Moments passed, framed by more blasts outside as jets raced overhead. K deflated in front of him. He stopped short of crying, but the tears were in his eyes. "You killed her!"

"What the hell are you talking about?" Even as he said the words, he wanted to vomit. Terre knew damned well it was true. Ali's blood might as well have been dripping from his hands. She wouldn't have stepped out onto the street if it weren't for him. He wasn't sure he was ready to admit it to K, though. Not yet.

"Ali is lying out there in a pool of her own blood, and you

don't even care! She wouldn't be dead if you hadn't run out there like a lunatic! You're not a bloody hero! What were you *thinking?*"

Not a hero.

"I was thinking there was a little girl sitting in a car ready to explode at any moment. What was I supposed to do? Sit and watch her die? Ali chose to come after me. I didn't ask her to."

"She went out there to save your ass!"

"My ass didn't need saving," he said indignantly, pushing K's hands away and giving him an extra shove. He relented from his aggression, though, his breathing already heavy and labored. "Krystal's did."

"It doesn't bother you that what you did killed the military officer assigned to protect us?"

"Ali went out there on her own." Terre's voice had lowered, the heat of his anger dissipating. "But yes, I do feel the guilt, if that's what you're asking. She's not the first to die because of my shortcomings." Tears were forming in his own eyes now, but he worked hard to push them down. There was no time for tears. His adrenaline had spiked so high that his voice quivered as he spoke. He waved his hand toward the window, as if K needed reminding of what was happening outside. "I'd change it if I could. I'm not heartless! But lots of people are dead. I can't help that now. I can sit here crying about Ali's death, or Cara's, or the dozens of people we watched fall into the bay—or I can help you get that program uploaded so we can stop anybody else from getting hurt. There'll be time to mourn later."

He had to push the burning in his gut aside; he'd be rendered completely impotent if he didn't.

K bit his lip, his eyes closed, and shook his head slowly.

"Listen, if you want to blame me, then blame me. But do it later. Right now, I want to stop these things." Terre risked a step forward. "I can't do it without you, K. I wouldn't know where to start."

K paused, his eyes focused on the floor. Sweat was beading on his forehead. The AC couldn't keep up with the abnormal July heatwave now that the large windows of the foyer were non-existent. K let the beads fall to the floor, his mop of black hair damp.

Terre was no less sweaty than his companion. It didn't matter that the temperature matched what they'd typically experienced in Guam. Ever since he'd had the nanobots injected, Terre seemed ready to perspire at the slightest exertion or increase in temperature.

"Let's go to my office." K didn't look back at Terre or give his words acknowledgement. Instead, he sauntered up to the elevator and slid his card through the reader.

K stepped inside before turning back toward Terre. His eyes were wet, angry, and pleading with him to end it. "Let's go!" He gestured to the space next to him.

Terre sighed and strode into the lift.

As the elevator dinged on their intended floor, the lights flickered, and the doors only opened a foot. Terre and K each took a side of the metal jaws, pushing the doors open enough for them to squeeze through.

They stepped out into an open bullpen office.

The lights had been left on, and a dozen or so laptops and computer displays were left unlocked. Mugs half-filled with coffee sat on desks, still steaming.

The lights flickered again, and then the room went silent as the power went out.

Sunlight streamed through the window, still providing ample light. The smell of burning metal hung in the air. Warm air whistled through the gaps where glass had broken and fallen away. It was impossible to tell if it was one of these missing glass panes that had plummeted below and struck Ali, but Terre shuddered all the same.

Smoke billowed from a nearby building, drifting inside before lingering over the technicians and the recently vacated desks. Sirens rang from somewhere below. Shouts from the street were audible through the open windows.

Terre tried to see if he could catch a glimpse of any drones flying by, but other than the haze of smoke, the skies appeared to be clear.

"Power outage will be a problem," he said.

"Yeah ..." K sighed, heading toward a cubicle at the back of the room.

"This is your office?"

The space was plain compared to several others nearby that held a more personal flare. A diploma from UC Berkeley hung from his cubicle wall in a nondescript frame, and a few hand-drawn anime characters hung beside it, with another one framed and propped up on his desk.

"I haven't had a lot of time here. As you may recall, I was hauled off to Guam, and then I was in rehab for the past six weeks.

"I don't even recognize most of the staff here anymore. Not that I spent a lot of time socializing when I was at my desk."

K booted up a laptop on his desk. A near-silent hum of the fan was barely audible above the wail of sirens from outside.

"Emergency backup power?"

"It's a laptop, Terre. But yeah, the internal network has its own reserve power. But the problem is, the network that connects to the AI won't be accessible while the power's out."

"That seems to be a flaw in the design."

"It's meant to connect to terraforming colonies, not psycho

killer war machines. A normal power outage wouldn't typically spell disaster. If the crops don't get watered for a couple of hours, the lives of thousands aren't hanging in the balance."

Terre watched as K opened a few folders on the device. "What are you doing?" he asked.

"I just want to make sure I've got everything on my hard drive. There's a lot of data here, but I think I've got everything. These are the programs for the Mars AI. They hold the commands for each of the units. Collectively, we call the protocols the Guardian Program. Most of the instructions are related to keeping the astronauts alive: small-scale terraforming for food development; protection from the outside vacuum of space; reproductive conditioning; habitat builds; repair and self-maintenance; that kind of thing. Anything you think you might need living in space. They can even adapt based on what's available around them. But their primary function is to keep humanity alive."

"So, explain to me again what this will do to these war bots?"

"I'm hoping, since the machines have more or less the same system, it will overwrite their killing programs and turn them into something designed to protect us from the vacuums of space."

"That won't cause its own set of problems?"

"Who knows, but at least they won't be killing us while we try to get them under control. If all I can do is buy us some time, it might just be enough."

Terre grabbed his phone and dialed Fredricks's number.

"Hoffman. What's your status?"

"Well, we've got some bad news. Ali's dead, sir."

K visibly tensed.

"What happened?"

"Part of K's office tower fell on her." Terre could hear how cold his own voice sounded, and he shuddered.

"Have you alerted anyone of her death?"

"There hasn't been much time to call it in. Consider this my official report. There were two Mountain View Police officers here moments after it happened. They shrugged it off. The roads are blocked. There's no way they're getting anyone out of here anytime soon."

"I'll deal with the paperwork from here. But to be honest, we've got a hell of a casualty list building. What about you and K?"

"K's downloading the program as we speak. The power's out here, though, so we'll need to get this to a place where we can upload it to the AI network. What's our next move?"

"It's likely gonna be out for the foreseeable future. We keep taking these things down, but more keep showing up. Thankfully, we haven't seen any more Onyx since this morning. But our standard drones are causing us enough grief. That being said, you wouldn't be able to upload to the Cloud from there, anyway. We can only make the connection through select secure devices. There's only one connection nearby that's still pinging the Cloud. You've got to get to UC Berkeley. Their robotics department designed this network, and they've still got an active connection, but like I mentioned this morning, you've got one shot. UC is Kristopher's alma mater; he should be able to get you to the right place. I'll let them know you're on your way, and they'll grant you whatever access you need."

"Understood. How are we getting there? There's no way we're driving."

"What happened to Rupert?"

"The pilot? What about the drones? They'll shoot us down!"

"We currently have an open window. Nothing has shown

on radar in the last twenty minutes. Get out of there PDQ. You have clearance to fly, but we don't know how long this window will last."

"Got it. We'll find our pilot and be on our way."

He hung up as K pulled a backpack out from under his desk. K grabbed his laptop and tossed it inside.

"I'm guessing we're on the move again? Where are we headed now?"

"Home sweet home. For you, anyway." Terre tapped the diploma on the cubicle wall. "UC Berkeley."

"It's been a while since I've called that place home." K grabbed his bag and walked to the elevator.

"We've got to find Gary." Terre followed close behind.

"I think he went to the basement with Alice and your rescue project."

"All right, then. Down we go."

Chapter Nine

Except for a lack of windows and the addition of a fitness center and daycare facilities, the basement didn't look much different from the floor above. It was comprised of large, open office spaces, green carpeting, a paneled ceiling, and several boardrooms. The florescent lighting had been shut off, and emergency lights lit the space, giving it an eerie feel.

Terre tried to get a glimpse inside the daycare, attempting to see how Krystal was faring, but there were too many kids laughing and climbing over each other. He was grateful the staff were keeping the kids entertained. How many of them would have no home or parents to go back to tonight?

Otherwise, the basement was buzzing. It appeared most of the staff who worked in the building had seriously heeded the call to take cover. The boardrooms overflowed as newcomers looked for a space to stand or sit.

Some looked angrily at their phones, indicating there wasn't any service, but Terre fought the urge to check his own to confirm his suspicion. Others just sat, staring at nothing, or chatting with each other as if it were just another coffee break on a regular workday.

Didn't these people take time off? Why were there so many staff at the office on a Saturday? Then he realized they still needed to take care of astronauts on the weekend.

Terre shook the distractions from his mind and

continued pushing through the crowd, trying to ignore the bits of conversation he heard as he made his way through.

They had to round a couple corners before he spotted their pilot leaning up against the back wall, staring at nothing and drinking from a flask.

Wonderful.

"Gary!" he called out.

The pilot took another sip from his flask before tucking it into an inside pocket within his leather jacket and closing his eyes.

"Come on, buddy. We've got to go."

Gary nearly choked on the mouthful of liquid as his eyes opened again, his pupils wide, as if realizing Terre was there for the first time.

"I'm not going anywhere. There's a battle waging in the sky out there! We're staying put until things clear up. I'm just a transport pilot. I'm not fighting or evading drones."

"Fredricks just let me know the skies are clear. We've got to go now before another assault comes."

"Sorry, but you'll need to find yourself another sap. I'm staying here." Gary took out his flask for another swig and wiped a droplet off his lip with the back of his hand.

K gave Terre a sideways glance and pulled him just out of earshot. "Do we really want this guy flying us anywhere?" he asked. "I, for one, would like to get there in one piece."

"Do you have any better options?"

"We could drive."

"Are you kidding? You saw the streets out there. We'd be better off walking. And besides, we don't have that kind of time."

"Well, it's either that or we die in a drunken fiery helicopter crash."

"Gary! How much have you had to drink?"

"What's it to you? I'm staying grounded."

"Dammit, Gary, you're still on the clock! You can either put that thing away and get us to Berkeley or I'll give Fredricks another call and let him know you're too drunk to do your duty."

The pilot cocked one eye open at him, weighing his options. "I don't believe you."

"Want to test me?"

Gary took another look around the room, probably gauging how many people would have to witness him with his tail between his legs. Nobody was paying the slightest attention to their argument.

"Fine." The flask disappeared back in his coat pocket.

His nostrils flared the entire way back to the stairwell. Once inside, his hand went to his forehead, and he took a few deep breaths. Winded or …?

"You all right there, captain?"

"Just gimme a minute."

K had already made his way up the first flight of stairs, hand also to his temple, Terre and Gary close behind. Terre couldn't tell if he was petrified, furious, or both. The fate of the world was riding on quite the ragtag team.

"When this is all over," Terre said, "I owe you both a beer."

They both shot him a look to shut up. He took the hint.

Terre didn't blame either of them for being on edge. He questioned his own sanity and resolve to stay as calm as he was.

The truth was, it wouldn't help him to panic. There'd be time for him to suffer panic attacks later, when this was all said and done. From driving off a collapsing bridge, saving a little girl, dodging drone attacks, and watching a colleague be dismembered by a falling windowpane, he had enough fuel to melt him into an agonized ball of self-pity.

But that had never been how he handled stress in the moment. Even traumatic stress. He needed to stay calm. The panic that welled up within him enabled him to keep laser-focused. Terre Hoffman had a task to complete.

Guilt was another matter. His guilt continued to bubble to the surface, picking away at him. He'd deal with it. But right now, he allowed it to fuel him.

For the moment, he was cool and calm, deflecting the serious with the odd, offhand sarcastic comment. That was more his speed. When their mission was over and he accepted the world had fallen apart, then he'd go on stress leave. Maybe he'd drink too much and gamble his savings away in Las Vegas for a weekend. He had been meaning to spend some time in Vegas for years. Self-destruct in the aftermath.

He didn't have time to deal with it now, though, and neither did these two. Too much was at stake for them to implode before completing the job before them.

"Listen, I realize this is not what any of us signed up for, but we have one job. If we can't get that program uploaded, then nothing will ever be the same again. I don't know about you, but I'm not ready to live in a post-apocalyptic wasteland with robot vacuums trying to kill us. Let's get this program delivered and then we can worry about the death-defying acts we overcame to get there.

"I'm sorry about Ali. If I could go back and do things differently …" He paused, considering, before shaking his head. "Well, I don't know if I would. I did what seemed right in the moment, and I got Krystal out of that vehicle. That's enough for me to sleep at night."

"That seems rather heartless," K piped up. His eyes were wet. He wasn't crying, but he was fighting back tears. He was taking Ali's death hard; harder than he could afford to in this moment.

"It is heartless. But that's what I need to be right now, to make sure that others don't meet the same fate as her. My actions as good as killed someone today. I'm going to need to figure out how to live with that."

It seemed like a long climb, but they eventually made it to the top.

The sun was descending as the afternoon faded into evening. Glows of reds, oranges, and yellows gave an ominous feel to the smoke-filled sky. Sirens continued to roar in the distance. How long would it take to repair the damage done today?

They boarded the helicopter, one fewer than when they'd arrived, and lifted into the evening sky.

Smoke dominated the surrounding buildings. Flames were being extinguished, but most of the towers would require months of repair, if not years, before they'd be fully operational again. Intriguingly, K's office tower had almost no damage when compared with those surrounding it. A few busted panes of glass seemed like inconsequential damage against gaping holes that spanned several floors and the flames that still glowed within chasms of neighboring facilities.

The flight over the Bay was even more telling. Pillars of smoke rose from dozens, if not hundreds, of locations across the entire area. Cars were backed up on every freeway within view, but whether they were being blockaded by authorities, wreckage, or sheer volume, Terre couldn't tell. Perhaps they were simply vacant; any automated system meant to deal with traffic congestion had been rendered useless.

K stared into the distance. Tears still welled in his eyes as he looked out the helicopter window.

The trip was quick. Who knew how long the same trip would have taken them over land? Hours to walk, at least. Traffic wouldn't be going anywhere anytime soon.

The other option would have been to commandeer a boat. The Bay was unsurprisingly empty. A few freighters were still coming in from the ocean, but nothing new was going out. Pleasure vessels that would have been out in full force on a regular Saturday in July were noticeably absent. By now, the Governor would have issued shelter in place orders for the entire area.

There was no way for them to tell what was happening at ground level, either. Among the vehicles he could see, emergency lights flashed, as well as National Guard units forcing their way through the gridlock.

Were there riots? Looting? Terre could only imagine full blown panic had taken over. Even if they did succeed, there was going to be a hell of a mess to clean up.

Terre now understood the hesitancy to just EMP the city. In one swift stroke, the detonation would neutralize the drones, but it would also take out the infrastructure that society had built their modern world upon. To be effective against the Onyx, the military would have to use NexGen3 EMP blasts. They'd knock out any shielding the bots had, but they'd also take everything else out for a hundred years, maybe more. And it wouldn't solve the problem—more bots would come. How much damage would be enough before the DOD made that call? Hopefully, it didn't come to that.

As they approached San Francisco, they could make out what remained of the city's downtown through a haze of smoke. The area had been decimated. Skyscrapers had fallen, and the drones had taken the Transamerica Pyramid out. Smoke still rose across the skyline, even though it must have been hours since the orbs had been defeated. Who knew how much havoc the standard drones had inflicted as well.

The flight only took fifteen minutes. They were already descending into Oakland, toward the Berkeley campus. The hills were still lush and green as they approached, despite the drought that had continued to strike the area. Oakland's streets were void of any traffic, aside from the police vehicles that were keeping them that way.

The Campanile tower still stood strong, making the campus' presence instantly discernible. Terre regretted that he had never made the trip up to the top of the clock tower on his several visits to the school. The view would never be the same.

They landed in Memorial Stadium on the east side of the campus. It was probably the nearest suitable location to land a helicopter at a university.

Having nobody around was a blessing. With everyone in lockdown, they didn't have to worry about interrupting practice or a game. They stepped out onto the field, and Gary clasped a sturdy hand on Terre's shoulder.

"I'm just going to wait here," he said, the smell of whisky still strong on his breath. Had he continued sipping from his flask while they were in the air? Too focused on the scenery during the flight, he hadn't taken the time to notice. He tried not to think about it.

That was one way to handle the end of the world. Terre just hoped they could find another way out of there; Gary wouldn't be flying anywhere else.

Hopefully, once they uploaded this program, it wouldn't matter.

He had his doubts, but he kept his mouth shut since he didn't have any better ideas.

K seemed convinced the bots would view the upload as an update, but who knew what the warmongers over at the Pentagon had done to K's machines? It was a long shot, at best, but it was all they had to work with.

"Let's go, K."

K reluctantly followed. Terre really needed him to snap out of it. When K had enrolled in his Computer Science class, he probably hadn't been expecting to come back after watching the city destroyed by killer robots, but he needed to hold it together a little while longer.

An empty parking lot awaited them outside the stadium. Long shadows and an unsettling silence filled the campus as they walked through the streets, punctuated by sirens in the distance and nearby shouts. Whether the exclamations were from students blowing off steam or shouts of fear, it was impossible to say. One thing was for sure: it was damn creepy to be walking through the deserted campus.

The tension was palpable, and at first, Terre wasn't entirely sure why. The campus was in one piece. From what they could tell from the air, the Onyx assault seemed to have stopped at the Oakland bridge. Perhaps it was the events of the day catching up to him—the effect of a nonstop thrill ride of destruction.

As they approached the campus' main hub, a half dozen terrified students ran in front of them. Of what, Terre couldn't see, but more yelling emanated from another part of the college grounds.

Something wasn't right here.

K stopped dead in his tracks. Sidewalks crisscrossed green spaces and ran between buildings. The area they stood in was wide open, with no protection from whatever the students had been running from. Regardless of what was happening, they couldn't stay. They'd be sitting ducks.

A grinding noise came from where the screams had originated moments before. The sound was foreign, but he could guess what was behind it.

Terre grabbed the blaster he'd been issued with back at base. He took a brief look at it. A little tutorial would have been handy. Hopefully, it was as foolproof as it looked.

"What are you doing?" K asked. He really was out of it.

"Did you not notice the screaming college students run past?"

"I did, but students are weird. It's likely a prank. What's the weapon for?"

"Those!" He gestured with the weapon held aloft.

A group of four of the humanoid robots Fredricks had showed them appeared at the edge of a brick building, far enough away that they had yet to notice the two technicians. The Sentinels marched across the school grounds. White-paneled armor covered their torso, blue accent lighting flickering in the darkness. Their heads looked to be covered in a synthetic skin, still pale white, but their empty eyes were haunting. They had weapons, too, similar to the one he held, and they began firing after the fleeing students.

K pulled out his weapon and aimed it at the machines.

"Not yet!" Terre hissed.

"What do you mean? They're chasing after those kids!"

"Yeah, and if you fire, they'll be chasing after *us*. I've already made enough of a mess today trying to be a hero."

K stood there, gun pointed, weighing his options. Would he be willing to see a few innocents get killed while he did what needed to be done?

Terre didn't blame him. How could he? He'd had to fight the same feelings as he'd jumped to save Krystal from the SUV. The urge to open fire on these Sentinels was difficult to resist.

But he had no idea how they'd react; no idea what their capabilities were. It was more likely they'd get themselves killed and end up helping nobody. Terre wasn't willing to die with that on his shoulders. Or worse, they would take the kids out, but the nanos would heal him and K. Too late to make a difference, they would be left only with the guilt of getting nothing done. They had to finish their mission first.

K was yet to be convinced. "How many, Terre?" he reasoned. "How many people have to die while we watch?"

"And how many more will die if we get ourselves killed

without uploading that program? We can get ourselves killed later. You want to save lives? You want to make sure Ali didn't die for nothing? You're the only one who can get this done."

K stood with his weapon drawn for another moment before he relented, bringing his arm down.

"Come on. We're almost there."

Chapter Ten

Terre and K skirted the outlying buildings as much as they could. Other than the students running from the Sentinel robots, there wasn't another soul on campus.

"What the hell are those bots doing here, anyway?" Terre asked, more thinking out loud than anything.

"They were designed here," K answered. "Well, their cousins—the Keepers—were, anyway. So, it doesn't surprise me there are a few of these on campus as well. Likely, the military has contracted some of the upgrades to the university. Why they have working weapons is beyond me, but my guess is they're studying the new modifications."

Neither of them had put away their weapons.

"Just hope there aren't any active in the lab," K said.

"There are some in the lab?"

"Does that surprise you?"

"I guess it surprises me that the university is working on military equipment."

"Brightest minds in the country. And they'll take the funding wherever they can get it."

Kristopher led them to the north end of campus, then continued on past what appeared to be its edge into a seemingly residential area.

"Where are we going, K? Is the lab off campus?"

"It's on the boundary. We're here, though."

The building was much more dated than Terre had expected. It looked closer to being an apartment than a state-of-the-art robotics lab. "What we're looking for is upstairs," he said.

Inside had been heavily renovated and was much cleaner than the complex's outward appearance. Glass casings and white tile gave the building the clinical look Terre had expected from the outside, but they weren't there for the aesthetics. They climbed the stairs cautiously. The less attention they could draw to themselves, the better, so they kept an ear open for signs of anything out of the ordinary.

They went up a few floors, maneuvered through a door, and then continued down an empty hallway until they stopped in front of what looked like a janitor's closet.

"This is where the network should be connected."

"You're kidding, right?"

Terre peered through a small window in the door. Cleaning supplies and storage filled a closet-sized room on the other side.

"You were thinking there would be a giant sign that says 'military network access'? On a campus full of college kids?"

"Point taken."

K pulled out a fob and held it to the receptor next to the doorway. The light on the console lit up red.

"Hmm."

"What does that mean?"

K tried the access again with the same result.

"I don't have clearance for this area."

A thought suddenly struck Terre. K sure knew a lot about what was going on at the university.

"So, did you know about this weapons program? You didn't know they were using your schematics on military equipment, did you?"

K, still facing the door, sighed, his shoulders slumping before he turned to him. He shook his head.

"I probably should have guessed, though. I knew that UC was assisting with the military robotics program. But remember, it's been a few years since I went to school here. A lot has changed. It's even possible the students don't know what they're working on. There are a lot of moving pieces to these things. They could just be working on the network, for all I know, but the Sentinels downstairs tell me they're more involved."

"So, what now?"

"We've got to find someone who can let us in."

He led them further down the hall. Windows into labs on either side showcased works in progress; robots in various stages of development. Some looked quite humanlike, even more so than the Sentinels. Some, Terre had to do a double take to make sure they weren't, in fact, human. Designers were getting skilled at emulating a more human look. Too good for Terre's liking.

It appeared the entire floor had been evacuated until they passed through a door into an open lab. Shattered glass lay strewn across the bodies of several students lying on the floor, either bleeding or sporting burn wounds that had completely pierced through them. Holes the diameter of a quarter had been ripped right through their bodies, leaving only cauterized flesh.

The Sentinels had been here.

K knelt on shards of glass that littered the floor as he put a hand down to a woman with wavy black hair. Bright red lipstick highlighted a pale face that had been lifeless for more than just a few minutes. Blood was everywhere. The lifeless eyes of students and researchers stared into nothingness.

"What have they done? Done to my friends? Done to my program?"

He wasn't crying. His voice didn't waver. Terre couldn't even sense anger. K said the words in a matter-of-fact manner, or maybe slightly bewildered. But a switch had flipped inside him, and Terre was worried he was edging toward the brink of madness.

"It's time." He stood up, grabbing a card connected to another fob from the curly-haired woman on the floor.

Something stirred in the corner. They both whipped around, weapons aimed.

A shrill shriek echoed across the lab, followed by a woman's panicked voice. "Don't shoot! Don't shoot!"

A light-skinned woman, with mascara smeared down her face and smudged purple eyeshadow that appeared to have once been ombre, sat on her haunches with her hands in the air, shaking uncontrollably. Terre and K simultaneously tucked their weapons away and ran to her side.

"It's okay!" Terre tried to keep his voice sounding soothing to calm her down, but he feared it came off as demanding. The woman, still shaking, placed her arms over her head in complete defensive mode. He lowered his voice to temper his tone. "We're not going to hurt you."

"Please … Please don't kill me." The woman was sobbing uncontrollably.

"Avery." K stepped forward, hands in the air, apparently familiar with the trembling woman. "Avery, it's me, Kristopher. And this is Terre. We're here to help."

She stole a glance upward, and for the first time, she truly saw them. Her sobbing didn't stop, but she wrapped her arms around K and held on as though he were a life preserver in the midst of a violent ocean.

"Kristopher!"

They gave her a moment. The sobbing tapered off, and Avery composed herself.

"The AI!" she cried. "Something activated them, and they

came through here and just started shooting at us! There was no warning. I was lucky I was in the bathroom! I hid and only came out when it had quieted down. But everyone was dead." Tears filled her eyes again, and K held her once more to provide her with the trivial amount of comfort he could.

"I know, I know." K held her tight. Terre suspected he needed the embrace just as much as she did.

He understood the compassion, but the bots were still on campus, wreaking havoc, and it would only be a matter of time before they made their way into the rest of the city as well. "Avery, why are these Sentinels hooked up to the Cloud?"

"There was never a reason for them not to be. We were testing connections; their responsiveness. They were only supposed to be able to turn on through a network command. There is no reason they should have been activated."

"It's not just here. Other AI units have been out of control. We're here to stop them."

"What happened? Has someone hacked them?"

K shook his head. "It's not a hack, but nobody's sure what the exact problem is. The units have just started turning themselves on and have stopped responding to control. The DOD is worried that any attempt to force connection will cause the AI to lock us out of the network completely."

"Why are you here? What are you going to do?"

"That's a long story, but we need to get into the military lab. We're going to upload the original Mars Guardian Program schematics we initially set up for terraforming colonists."

She looked at him, thinking for a moment. "They'll think you're sending a rollback to an earlier version," she said, putting the pieces together on her own. "Their programming shouldn't sense that anything is amiss."

"That's what I'm hoping, at least."

Avery closed her eyes and took a few deep, calming breaths. She tugged on the bottom of her white button-down shirt, straightening it out.

"Okay, I'll let you in. But I had nothing to do with any of this."

They walked back toward the locked door. Her fob hovered over the receiver, and the panel clicked green. Terre hesitantly entered what still appeared to be a janitor's closet.

At the back of the tiny closet, the wall twisted and opened up into another room. The open section was still small, but it was large enough to hold the desk space needed for a setup of computers and monitors. More like a military operation. The room itself was empty except for a few slick-looking computers, several high-resolution monitors on a desk, and five more on the wall. A few charts and graphs hung around the room, impossible to decipher at a glance.

"This is it?" Terre asked.

"This is it."

"Do you have a network cable around here, Avery? I've got the program on my laptop."

"You're not going to be able to connect that to the network. This computer," she said, pointing to one of the four set up against the back wall, "is the only one with the connection you need. That's it. It's stonewalled to any other IP."

"What options do we have for loading this thing, then?"

"USB?" Terre offered.

"You'll never find one big enough. We're talking about petabytes of information. Unless..."

K pulled the laptop from his backpack and set it on the desk, then he took out a set of computer tools and started cracking the case open.

"What the hell are you doing?"

"Trust me. Avery, can you scrounge up a USB Peripheral Controller for me?"

"Great idea! I think I can find one."

She took off out of the room.

"Do you want to explain to me what your plan is?"

K had detached a block of circuits from his device and was continuing to unscrew the remainder of the periphery attached to it. "I'm going to turn my hard drive into a USB plug," he said.

"Of course!" Terre stammered.

"Aren't you a network specialist? I'm surprised you didn't think of it."

He cringed. *Why didn't I think of that?* "I'm sure I would have got there."

"Sure." K flashed him a smile. It was nice to see a bit of the old K still shining through, even if it was at his expense.

Avery returned, out of breath. "I've found one I think you should be able to use," she said. "But you'd better hurry. I swear I can still hear gunfire somewhere in the building."

"Any chance that door's bulletproof?" Terre asked.

"Can you think of any reason a university would have installed a bulletproof door?" Avery remarked.

"Killer robots?"

"Quiet, you two," K snapped. "I need to concentrate. I've never really done this before, and if I destroy my hard drive, this will all be for nothing."

"Lips are sealed." Terre made a zipper motion over his lips as he pressed them together, which earned a suppressed laugh from Avery.

Good. Anything he could do to take her mind off the carnage outside.

"Anything we can do to help?" Avery decided it was worth testing the silence.

K didn't look up. "Just let me focus. I'll let you know if I need anything else." He ran a hand through his thick black hair. "Maybe watch the door."

Back in the fake janitor's closet, Terre pressed his face to the small window that faced the outside hall. The smell of cleaner was overpowering. Paper towels, cleaning cloths, deodorizers, and tools stacked the steel shelves lining the walls. Handles of mops and brooms jutted out into the space, threatening to poke him in the ribs if he didn't watch his step. No detail was spared in ensuring that from the outside, the room appeared legitimate. But within its deep recesses lay a connection to one of the most powerful military networks in the world.

"Actually, Avery," K piped up, "if you could make sure we still have access to the network through this computer, that would be one less thing to think about."

Avery nodded and moved over to the workstation. Terre could tell she was glad for the distraction, but her entire concentration wasn't with them. He would have to keep an eye on her if things went south. She wasn't fit to make decisions in this state. Hell, was *he* in any better of a position? He guessed you did what you had to do. They had all lost people close to them, and it was just as much her fight as it was his.

The three sat in silence for ten minutes as K soldered what remained of his laptop and Avery clicked keys on the computer beside him. Terre felt mostly useless as he peered out into the empty hallway, his heart racing with every flicker of the lights or creak of the wall.

"All right. The moment of truth," K said, standing up with his newly mutated device. "I hope I didn't fry anything."

He inserted the newly attached USB device into the single port the desktop offered. The board from the laptop sticking out of the drive seemed almost comical, but they weren't going for aesthetics.

"Okay," he said, taking a seat on the solitary chair in the room. "It looks like it worked. We ready on the network side of things, Avery?"

"As good as we're going to get," she said. Her lips curled in a smile, but her tired eyes betrayed them.

K took her spot at the workstation. He punched a few commands into the terminal and held his breath. "Okay!" he announced after a few moments had passed. "We're in. Program uploading. Cross your fingers, everyone."

Terre, still sitting in the closet, glanced back to the workroom. Multiple monitors had come to life on the desk. The five displays set up on the wall above the machines had also turned on, each revealing separate sets of the Sentinel robots, all dormant. Two displays were set to close-ups of storage banks housing four or five of the humanoid machines. The center display revealed what looked to be a warehouse full of them. There had to be hundreds.

"Are these all showing the same location?" Terre's mouth hung open as he studied the screens. He was afraid of what the answer would be.

"No," Avery replied.

"I bet you'll also tell me these aren't all of the locations, either."

"You'd be right on that one, too. They've got these things spread out across the country. They have them in storage in California, Texas, Florida, New York. All over."

"You didn't believe Fredricks?" K piped up.

Terre shook his head. "It's not that. It's just different to see a robot army with your own eyes."

The images on the screens haunted him. A warehouse full of robot warriors, all sleeping, all potentially able to wake up at any moment and start shooting anything that moved. They should destroy them now, but the almighty dollar dictated that they should try to salvage them instead.

Any science fiction movie he had ever seen told Terre this was the wrong way to go.

He hoped he was wrong.

"How long is this going to take, K?"

"A lot longer if you keep interrupting me."

Terre peered out the window into the hall, continuing to glance back at the screens. Nothing happened on either front, which was a relief, but it also made the minutes drag on.

The terror of the slaughter outside was only a fraction of what Terre imagined his wife and daughter must have gone through the night of the attack. If he had only chosen a different path, would they still be with him today? Would he be somewhere other than a computer lab, hidden in a janitor's closet, trying to save the country from their own rogue machines? Maybe someone else would be standing here today instead of him. Or maybe not. Maybe there was a destiny to the decisions one made; an unalterable path written in the stars.

"Terre!" Avery's commanding voice spoke through his thoughts.

He snapped out of his daydream and looked at her in a daze.

"Can you see what it is?" she whispered. "What's moving in the hall?"

He hadn't even noticed the footsteps coming from the other side. He peered out the closet window in time to see the white-paneled backside of a Sentinel exiting toward the stairwell, its blue lights casting a glow through the hall until the stairwell door shut behind it.

"It was a Sentinel. I think it's gone, though." He pressed his face against the pane to get a better look and held his breath, trying to see if there were others.

He lowered his voice to nearly a whisper. "I can't tell if there are more. How's it going over there, K?" he asked.

Kristopher was still gazing at the screen. There was nothing for him to do at this point but watch the progress bar. They had the fastest connection available, but it was still a crawl, given the sheer size of the files they were trying to install.

"Ten more minutes. Maybe. We're about halfway there."

The glass window in the doorway shattered, and Terre instinctively jumped away as a white robotic fist punched its way into the room. He pulled up his blaster and fired through the opening.

He missed his mark and etched a hole in the wall across the hall. There was no sign of the Sentinel that the arm had been attached to.

Avery leapt back, rolling under the computer table, hiding beside K's feet.

"Whatever's happening back there," K yelled from his workstation, "you need to deal with it! We need more time!"

K hadn't moved from the desk, muttering both disparaging and encouraging words at the screen.

Aside from the clicking of keys and Avery's muted sobs, the room was now still. Terre froze, anticipating the next wave of assault. With his CD-115 aimed through the window, he resisted the urge to stand up to check the hall with every fiber of his being.

The door came flying off its hinges. Terre spun around as the Sentinel flew toward him, barely in time to take the brunt of the impact on his shoulder. It pushed him to the ground, knocking the blaster from his hand.

Avery screamed as the sound of crashing metal reverberated through the room.

Terre lifted the door off himself, pushing it into the room

and using its heft to plow into a pair of Sentinel robots as hard as he could manage.

The blunt force pinned them to a wall before pressing their bodies against the sides of a desk. Terre couldn't see anything behind the door as he leaned his body into their frames. He had caught them off guard with the element of surprise, but he could tell it wouldn't be good enough to hold them for long.

K stood from the desk, blaster in hand, and fired at point blank range, into the one of the robot's necks, and then the other. Synthetic flesh peeled away from where the blaster bolts made impact, melting away from the robotic metal beneath.

The Sentinels stopped resisting against the panel Terre held against them, but that didn't slow K's efforts. Their faces were vulnerable to the blasts, but sparks flew off the robust paneled armor that covered their torsos as the blaster fire struck, less penetrable to its force. If there had been any question as to whether they were going to stand back up, K removed any trace of it. By the time his weapon stopped firing, the robots were unrecognizable.

Movement caught Terre's eye at the edge of the room. There were more Sentinels in the closet. Terre could make out the edges of at least four, but there had to be more behind the wall.

K sat back down at the desk, frantically working on the computer that had surprisingly remained intact after the previous skirmish. The progress bar on the upload showed there were several minutes until completion.

Fresh blaster fire echoed through the room. The bots were coming, and there were more of them than he was going to be able to handle on his own. Even if K was able to fully divert his attention from the upload, it wasn't an even match.

Terre scrambled to where his blaster had fallen to the floor, grabbed it, and fired a few shots before taking cover, narrowly dodging being blasted away himself. They were trapped in a box of a computer lab with who knew how many robot soldiers besieging them.

They wouldn't get out of the room alive.

Avery continued to crouch behind the desk, with no way to defend herself. Terre ejected several more rounds of firepower into the approaching units. He was barely managing to cover K, whose back was turned to the attackers, the computer he worked feverishly at his sole point of focus.

They weren't going to survive much longer. If his allies perished in this fight, it would be two more dead, plus himself. Two more dead because of his inaction.

There was only one thing he could do.

The CD-52 Drone Surge he had received at the lab still hung against his back. Its weight had largely gone ignored for the bulk of the day, but now it called to him, sensing its time had come. Samantha had told him it had a range of a dozen yards, so it would take out the handful of soldiers in front of him and hopefully any more that remained in the hall.

There was only one problem.

"What are you doing with that?" K yelled, grabbing his own blaster and firing at the doorway, using the desk as cover from the stray fire. "You're going to kill the upload!"

"We don't have a choice! They're going to kill us!"

And they'd likely destroy the computers in the process, anyway, but he didn't have time to explain himself. He lifted the weapon to his shoulder. He wished he would have been able to have had a practice round, but he closed his eyes and hoped for the best, moving the CD-52 and his shoulder around the corner and into the line of fire.

His movement knocked over the door he had been using

as a shield and revealed the white demons swarming into the room.

Without responding to K, Terre squeezed the trigger.

As he did so, movement on the monitors on the wall caught Terre's eye. Hundreds of robot eyes lit up. They were coming online. Every single one of them. Life had found each of the formally dormant bodies.

Warmth erupted from the weapon he held and then it became ice cold. Its own hum fell silent in Terre's grip.

All the room's monitors winked out, everything going black as the power flipped off. Silence overcame them as the weapons fire ceased. White Sentinel bodies powered down and stood inactive, their destructive force rendered inoperative.

A steady and slowing whir, indicative of a computer powering down, followed.

"NOO!!" Terre winced as K screamed.

Avery's controlled breathing and the panting of the two men were the only noises left as the hum of the lights, displays, and other electronics on the floor winked out, leaving the laboratory in near total darkness.

Terre sat there, trying to catch his breath, as K buried his face in his palms.

"This may be a stupid question," Terre said, "but is there any chance the upload worked before the weapon killed it?"

"The upload wasn't complete." K replied. Terre couldn't see his colleague in the darkness but could hear the dismay in his voice. "They only got half the program. What parts they received, I can only guess. It might only have been the base functionality they already have."

"I'd say it doesn't look promising," Avery chimed in. "Did you see the eyes of those things light up?"

"Yeah." Terre swore. The monitor still held the imprint of the shining blue eyes. So many eyes, and they were spread all across the country, including more on campus. If the program had indeed not uploaded, they were going to find out soon. "Either way, we can't stay here. Let's go."

Terre kept his weapon drawn as they stepped into the hall.

Chapter Eleven

"These kids shouldn't be out here." Terre stepped out onto the campus grounds, K and Avery behind him.

Groups of students had filtered out of wherever they had been hiding, most wide-eyed and cautious about each step they took into the green spaces between the main campus buildings. Light murmurs echoed among them as they looked to each other with both solace and curiosity. Mostly, they were silent. Terre imagined the shock of the evening's events would have been enough to traumatize even the most resilient among them. Other than the bodies in the lab, Terre had no sense of how many the Sentinels had killed, nor did he know how long they had been on campus. But even one life taken was too many and would be enough to define your entire university experience. And they weren't even sure if it was all over yet. Not to mention the assault on the city they must have witnessed from across the bay.

Light from the full moon reflected the uncertainty on the faces of the students. Many continually glanced over their shoulders, unconvinced the threat had passed. Bags under red eyes marked those who had been crying, and tears still lingered in the eyes of others—tears of both fear and mourning.

The rest of the campus was also dark. The blast from Drone Surge wouldn't have been powerful enough to have knock out power much further than the server room, so there must have been another cause for the outage. Dread filled Terre as his mind scrambled to think of a possible cause. None he could come up with were good, but he did his best not to jump to any conclusions.

The fact that the students had ventured out into the night told Terre that, although hesitant, the students *did* believe the threat had passed. He didn't believe they'd venture out of the dark buildings simply because of a power outage if it meant being led into slaughter.

"Where are the bots?" he whispered to his companions.

The question hung unanswered. Of course, nobody with him had any more information than he did. The lack of blaster fire and screaming was a positive sign that the Sentinels had at least stood down, but the chill that ran down his spine told him it was a false reprieve. He held onto his standard blaster, the Drone Surge hanging impotent on his back, its single charge expelled. The metal of the weapon still felt ice cold, to the point of discomfort. K followed suit by his side, afraid that the tide might shift at any moment. Avery trailed behind them, eyeing her peers as they streamed toward the center of campus, as stunned as they were.

Those wandering the lawn seemed to be all headed in a single direction. As they passed back into the main center of the campus, the central green space held nearly a hundred students, gathered in a circle around something Terre wasn't yet able to see.

He was prepared to make an educated guess, though.

Terre pushed his way past the students loitering in his way. A few protested, and a few others gave him a dirty look, but he ignored them all.

Four deactivated Sentinels stood frozen in the center of the commotion, standing still, their backs to one another in a bizarre display, as if each had picked a compass point and stood on guard before deactivating. The spectators stood about a dozen feet back in a circle, all curious but still uncertain of the machines.

"K! Get over here!" Terre kept his voice as hushed as was possible over the gawking students. He wasn't sure why he was hesitant to raise his voice, other than it felt as though the somber mood around them called for it.

"What's the deal with these things?"

K walked toward the frozen bots, stopping a few feet short. "They're rebooting. We need to get the students out of here."

Terre didn't hesitate before shouting, "Everyone get back! Get inside! These robots could activate at any moment!"

Questions of uncertainty buzzed through the crowd. A few turned, but most didn't move.

"*Now!*" Terre yelled, unconsciously waving a palm at them, not realizing he still had his blaster in hand until he was mid-swing.

Subdued shrieks and urgent chatter replaced the hesitancy, and those in the crowd turned and scattered into the night.

"How long will it take?"

K shook his head. "When we run a standard update on the Mars bots, it's fifteen, twenty minutes tops. We run most of the updates while the colonists are sleeping, though, so the units really get a full six-hour recharge. We could have minutes or hours. But I'd err on the side of caution."

"So, what do we do with them?" Avery chimed in. "We can't just let them reboot!"

Terre lifted a weapon to the head of the bot closest to him.

"Wait," Avery interjected. "Are you sure there's no other way? What if the upload did what we needed?"

Terre hesitated. "Do we really want to take that chance?

I'm working under the assumption we're going to have four killer robots three feet in front of us within the next five minutes," he said. "If the upgrade did what we hoped, which I doubt, we can repair them. If we stand around here talking about it for a minute too long, they'll shoot us instead. I'm not prepared to take responsibility for that." Terre turned an eye to K. "Are you?"

K didn't bother answering and lifted his weapon.

"Aim for the neck," K said. "Their skull is too heavily armored. Their neck holds just as much vital circuitry, but is more susceptible to damage."

Terre fired a charge at the neck of the north-facing Sentinel and it collapsed. He repeated the action on the one facing west. K took out the other two.

"Hopefully there aren't many more running around."

"I don't think we need to worry about that now," K responded. "If it didn't work, we'll have bigger problems than a few loose droids on campus."

"There you idiots are!" Gary's voice echoed through the night. He was muttering something to himself that Terre couldn't make out.

He faltered a bit in his step as he made his way over. Terre cursed under his breath; the fool probably hadn't put away the drink since they'd arrived. He knew everyone had different ways of dealing with stress, but Gary was their ride, their ticket back to Treasure Island, and the man was barely fit to walk, never mind fly an aircraft.

"We've gotta get outta here!" their pilot stammered.

"We do, but you're in no condition to fly."

"Who said anything about flyin'? No. I've tracked down a boat for us."

"A boat?" That sounded better than being in the air if it was possible the bots could reboot at any moment. "That's brilliant! But I'm not letting you drive that, either," said Terre.

"Yeah, I'm brill-iant. There'd be no way they'd be gettin' me in the sky again with those … robots shooting at everything."

Terre grabbed Gary by the arm. "Lead the way."

The walk to the marina took about an hour from the campus. It was mostly downhill, so other than trying to keep Gary standing upright, it wasn't a difficult walk.

They approached the docks under the light of the full moon. The night air sent a chill through Terre. Orange glows reflected off the otherwise dark water, showcasing the fires that had yet to be put out around the bay. Seagulls cawed through the night sky, and the spotlight of an occasional helicopter circled the tendrils of smoke that still floated upward.

Any slight amount of reprieve was welcome. Terre resisted the urge to close his eyes and let sleep overtake him. Visions of a warm bed taunted him as he trudged forward, each step on the descent to the water threatening to bring him down. With no way of knowing if they had succeeded or failed, they had to make as much ground back to base as possible.

The rest of the company, with the exception of Gary, carried on in silence. Other than the flames that had yet to be tempered down, a few helicopters circling, and a variety of emergency boats scouring the bay, the surrounding city was completely dark, void of city lights as far as they could see.

But how long would the ceasefire last?

When the bots rebooted, would they be friendly? Or still bent on their destruction?

Terre repeatedly scanned the sky for signs of the bots' return. Every helicopter that passed, every bird that flew by, sent his pulse racing. Terre feared the AI had detected their actions and shut down everything they could. What would they do if they were locked out of the power grid altogether?

Whether what they had done would show any level of success, only time would tell.

Terre just wanted to be done with it all. His idea of a stressful day had previously comprised of a crashed server or when the threat of a network hack became too real for comfort; planes falling from the sky and secret robotic soldiers shooting at him were far more than he was prepared to deal with.

K's eyes surveyed the sky as well, carefully monitoring the helicopters and their path around what remained of the Bay area. By the way he fidgeted with the weapon in his holster, Terre could tell what he was thinking. K wasn't convinced the upload had achieved anything.

"The eyes, Terre," he'd blurted out as they made their way down University Avenue toward the marina. "They turned on when they detected a threat within the network. Those bots are programmed to attack when that happens."

"But what would their reaction be if the upload was successful?"

K shook his head and rubbed a fidgety hand through his hair towards the back of his neck. "It was incomplete."

"I know it was incomplete," Terre replied. "But what's the best-case scenario? Pretend for a minute it was a hundred percent complete. What would you expect the reaction of the Mars robots to be?"

K's eyes danced back and forth as he played out scenarios in his head. "It's hard to say. The Sentinels were never part of the Mars program. If they were Keepers, their program would be to care for the children in the settlements, to act as companions if needed, and provide protection for those in their charge."

"So, it's likely that the reality remains somewhere between those two extremes. Destruction of an enemy and the protection of people. Maybe they'll just stand down enough that we can work out another solution."

"There are too many variables. If the upload wiped the entire old program before uploading the new bits, then ..."

"Then we wouldn't have gotten anything done without activating the safeguards. You designed them this way for a reason."

"Ugh! I know! I just wish I knew what parts of the programming they received. We have no idea what we're up against."

Terre stopped, and K slowed to meet his gaze. He grasped K's shoulder. "If nothing else, you bought us time," he said. "These choppers can survey the damage, and hopefully rescue those stranded or buried in the rubble."

"I just hope we didn't make things worse."

If anyone made anything worse, Terre thought, *it was me, firing that EMP weapon in the lab before the upload was complete.*

Terre kept his thoughts to himself for the moment, though; he had to process the events of the evening, and he knew that had he not fired the weapon, they'd all be dead. There was no sense in worrying about something that hadn't happened yet.

As they boarded the boat Gary had procured at the marina, the smoke rising in the distance continued to garner his attention. Like a moth to a flame, the devastation was horrific, but Terre couldn't bring himself to look away. How many people had died before they were able to upload the program? How many more lives would be changed forever?

For now, the city lay wounded, unable to deal with the what-ifs that might come if the bots were to spring to life again. But for the moment, at least, the people of San Francisco could breathe.

Terre didn't want to think about how much worse things could get.

Waves crashed around the bowrider as it sped over the Bay toward Treasure Island. The frequency of choppers flying overhead continued to increase as the minutes ticked by. Terre consciously checked his watch as the shoreline of Berkeley disappeared behind them. By the time the boat had left the dock, a solid twenty minutes had passed from the incident in the lab.

As they reached their destination, it appeared that the threat had been diffused, at least for the evening.

Eventually, even the helicopters quieted down for the night. The evening air was permeated only by the sounds of crickets chirping, waves crashing, and the shouts of those in the city still trying to douse flames or prevent looters from taking advantage of a city in chaos.

"Well," Terre said, placing a hand on K's shoulder. The kid stiffened, the lean muscles of his shoulder already seemingly wound up in knots. "It looks like it's worked. Well enough to stop the attacks, at least."

K didn't answer right away, his gaze still lost on the emptiness of the bay, and the efforts of the clean-up on its shores. K had said nothing during the entire boat ride. None of them had. The weight of anticipation had been heavy among all of them, other than Gary, who had passed out the moment the boat left the dock.

Avery had been the only one among them who had ever piloted a boat, and she had offered to ferry them back to base. She was currently being questioned by the officers who had welcomed them upon arrival.

There were still several lights from the Coast Guard that continued to light up the water, particularly in the areas where the bridges had collapsed. After a full day, it was unlikely they'd be finding any more survivors, but Terre could see the bloated, lifeless forms being hauled upon their decks in the harsh lights they cast upon the water.

Too many civilians had died. Too many families had been torn apart. The blood that coursed through his veins scratched at his insides, raw and tingling, as the effects of the adrenaline rush that had filled his entire day finally began to subside.

He grabbed the robot pendant, still hanging from his neck, and silently prayed he'd never have to see such an artificial insurgence again. He knew deep down the situation wasn't over, but he needed to hope that it was, even if it was only for the evening.

Epilogue

Kristopher Klein sat on the edge of Treasure Island, watching as emergency crews worked to dampen the flames that still glowed through the windows of offices and homes across the Bay. The Coast Guard didn't stop throughout the night, pulling people in from the water. Against all odds, not all those who entered the water became casualties. Some had managed to cling to the pilons that remained standing, clinging for hours, wondering if they'd ever be safe again, until the passing Coast Guard patrols finally pulled them on board.

Sleep evaded him. Every time K closed his eyes, he could only see images of the dead in the robotics lab. Most of them were students, merely trying to master a profession they had hoped would give them a future. A future now stolen from them.

It was nearly impossible to know the full impact the upload would make on the server, but he knew it was incomplete. A standard reset would have given them less time before the bots returned to the streets and the skies, so he guessed he had to be thankful for that. The upload had been slightly more substantial than a reset; if it hadn't, the sound of blaster fire would still be echoing in the streets, instead of just inside his head.

However, gunshots now followed the screams. It

appeared that the biggest threat to the people of San Francisco was now themselves. Protests had already filled the streets before the attack. The large segment of the population who had lost jobs due to automation and robotics were already struggling for survival. A decimated downtown was only going to make things worse, as was apparent from the cries of looters and those taking advantage of a catastrophic situation. It was hard to say how the city would recover—if it ever would.

And that was only if the military's bots didn't come back.

Which they would.

K had given his briefing to Fredricks and a senior official, whose name K couldn't pronounce, never mind remember. All he could do was warn them. The fix was temporary. If they were lucky, it would buy them some time; weeks, at the most. It was K's best guess that the bots were recalibrating their systems, integrating the successful parts of the upload and ignoring the incomplete bits. They had been designed to adapt to their programming; to evolve past inefficiencies.

To learn.

The best course of action was to get access to their operating network now that they were dormant and shut the whole lot of them down.

He could see in the official's eyes that that option was not on the table. They'd try to gain access and regain control; to work with their current specialists to deter the actions from repeating themselves. Find out what went wrong.

K shook his head. *What went wrong was you built artificially intelligent war machines and they did what you designed them to do. Kill.*

The only question now was what K would do. Before today, he had never seen death, and now his vision was clouded with images of one dead body after another.

It was rare for him to connect with anyone. He enjoyed

being a loner, locking himself in his room and figuring out the next line of code.

He knew that was why it felt as though his insides had been ripped out as he saw Ali lying in the street, her eyes open, glass shards embedded in her. He couldn't shake the image, or the emptiness he felt.

The ball in his stomach felt painfully real and yet utterly ridiculous. He had just met Ali, but the rarity of the connection made it feel as though he had known her for a lifetime. A spark that had rarely been lit glowed for those few hours.

And it was all over after one brash move.

If he was honest, only part of him blamed Terre for her death. His actions had been the cause, but he struggled to reconcile the act of altruism in rescuing Krystal from the van and the result of Ali being impaled. He knew deep down Terre had done the right thing, but it didn't make it hurt any less.

Being alone was how he typically operated. It was how he architected the NASA program—mostly by himself. Teams actioned what he had discovered, but the bones of the Guardian Program had been his.

What was he now to do with the program after it had been bastardized, now that it no longer resembled the barbs of protection and community he had pieced together? It didn't help that he didn't know the outcome of the partial upload; to what extent would the bots be on a mission to kill or to protect. He only knew it wouldn't be enough.

Edges of morning were showing themselves on the horizon, casting light on a city blemished by an unholy wrath. In the coming days, K knew there would be some that declared this to be God's judgment on a species who themselves were trying to play God. And maybe they were right.

Maybe it was inevitable for man to suffer for their own stupidity. The fall of humanity would be brought about by manipulating powers they didn't fully understand. Creating weapons outside of their understanding and their refusal to deactivate those machines was testament to the fact that humanity wasn't ready to be the gods they sought to be.

Did K himself have any right to save humanity from itself? Or should he disappear into the jungle and pray his days would run out before the plague man had unleashed reached him? He had no ties to this world; his family had abandoned him long ago. He had been married to his work, and now it seemed that he'd pay for gifting humanity with something they weren't yet ready for.

All he knew was that the next day, he would terminate his contract. He wouldn't play advisor to those who didn't want to hear his advice. If he were to play any part in stopping the destruction of civilization, he would once again need to go it alone.

If not, Kristopher Klein would be condemning all of humanity to pay for his sins.

ARTIFICIAL INSURGENCE

Six weeks after the attack on San Francisco, the United States has returned mostly to normal. Traumatized by his experience Terre Hoffman, seeks some recovery in Las Vegas before starting a new position in the private sector.

However, when technology begins to malfunction on the Strip, he quickly realizes the threat is not yet over, and is reluctantly pulled back into action when he learns that Kristopher might be up to something mysterious in the Nevada desert.

Order your copy today.

Keep reading for a sneak preview

ARTIFICIAL INSURGENCE

HERMAN STEUERNAGEL

THE TERRE HOFFMAN CHRONICLES | BOOK TWO

Chapter 1

Annika

Las Vegas Convention Center — 2052

It wasn't the heat of the Las Vegas Convention Center that caused beads of sweat to drip down Annika Phillips's forehead. Thankfully, the building had air conditioning. It was mid-September in the desert city, and without the steady stream of cool air blowing through the auditorium, Annika likely wouldn't have made it through her presentation. Instead, it was the two thousand people in attendance of her lecture on building human relationships in banking which caused her to perspire. The audience was comprised of a mixture of virtual spectators and physical attendees.

Annika had given presentations before, over video conferencing and in front of her own staff, but never to such great numbers. Annika had successfully managed to stifle her fears for the bulk of the lecture. She had refined her delivery through multiple rehearsals, but the glazed look on the faces of the online attendees told her most weren't even paying attention.

Everything had played out exactly as she had expected. But with the question and answer session coming up, her inner imposter syndrome was rearing its ugly head.

"This is why," Annika said, composing herself, "despite the technological advances in Artificial Intelligence over the past decade, humanity will not be rendered obsolete. We provide relationships that people crave. Regardless of advanced algorithms designed to help our clients discover adequate products, there will always be a significant portion of the population who will want a human face to deliver options to them."

As she paused, a message popped up on the screen projected through her eye-piece. Annika cursed at not having turned her notifications off for the lecture, but she was thankful nothing else had come through until the end.

Her heart stopped for a split second at the name displayed with the message: *Cheyenne.* Her sister knew she was presenting today, and Annika worried that something was wrong, until she read the message.

Can we go up the Eiffel Tower for supper? I want to see the fountains when they're lit up.

Annika breathed a sigh of relief. Of course, the teenager was okay. She had to remind herself that Ember was keeping watch over her. If anything had been wrong, the bot would have alerted her. Monitoring Cheyenne was the whole reason they had brought the bot along; the whole reason they had received it to begin with.

Her younger sister was waiting alone in their room for Annika to be done, as she had been all day. Just as she had done for the past three days during Annika's conference on human-centric banking. Cheyenne had seemed fine with the arrangement, but being stuck in a hotel room with only a bot and homework for company was bound to get old fast. Understandably, the girl was eager to spend some time on the Strip.

An evening overlooking the Bellagio fountains sounded like a great way to end their Vegas experience, but her sister would have to wait until Annika wasn't standing in the middle of a presentation before she agreed to it.

Annika regained her focus and cleared her throat.

"Any questions?"

Nearly two hundred people sat in the theater-style rows that filled the conference room, and another two thousand watched remotely. Their faces scrolled by in her eye-piece. Most sat in their home offices, while others were in coffee shops; there were even some on beaches. It seemed there were almost more digital nomads than those with a permanent address. When there was no telling what industry would collapse next, and with most of their work being virtual, there was no point in being fixed in any one location, other than for tax benefits. Countries that were ahead of the curve had been smart enough to implement a universal basic income before large swaths of jobs disappeared, retaining the presence of their workforce. Almost nobody in Annika's field kept an office in a physical branch anymore.

Most of the attendees were bankers, customer care advisors, or those on the ground, working directly with clients. But Annika's role was in the back office: she worked alongside the employees of different banking institutions to ensure they felt validated in their field.

This was the second time Annika had traveled to the city of Las Vegas on business. She had attended so many of these conferences virtually from her own home in Saskatoon. Being home had its benefits, but it was hard to pass up the opportunity of getting to present in person.

Her employer, the Canadian Human Banking Association, had agreed to pay part of the cost of the trip once the conference organizers had approached her to be a guest speaker. The work she had been doing for the CHBA had put her at the forefront of human-centered banking over the course of the past decade. Although AI powered most of the banking industry, there was still a big role for staff to play in maintaining face-to-face relationships with their customers, offering someone to answer questions about investing, loans, and banking in general with a warmth and intuition that only a human could provide. Much of the CHBA's client base still preferred to speak to a human over an AI interface. Though, as much as Annika was being paid to say otherwise, as bots improved in their ability to emulate conversation, compassion, and warmth, the days of human-centric banking were rapidly coming to an end.

"Have you seen the latest models from Cyber Dynamics?" said a suited man sat in the front row. He was in his late twenties, slightly overweight, and clean-shaven, with drooping eyes that betrayed he had stayed out a bit later than he should have the previous night. "Their advancements are supposed to make their interactions almost indistinguishable from a human."

Colby was his name. He worked for the CHBA as well and was technically her superior.

What's he after? Annika thought. *Is he hoping to make me look stupid in front of all these people?*

Whether or not his point was valid, the entire aim of the conference was to assure the attendees they weren't headed for obsolescence.

She had to remember all eyes were on her, so she couldn't openly scoff or berate him for undermining her presentation. If it were anyone else, she'd believe it could be an honest question. With Colby, though, he always had an ulterior motive, likely one to serve his own interests.

He slumped in his chair and carried himself smugly, confirming her suspicions. Though he was young, Colby thought he knew the finance world better than those who had been in it for decades longer. An early promotion to a lofty position while others twice his age were being laid off probably hadn't eased the stroking of his ego. Annika wondered how he had pulled it off. She had certainly worked with Colby long enough to know it wasn't based on competency. The only thing she could come up with was that it was cheaper to promote someone with less experience for a smaller paycheck.

She wished they would have chosen someone who didn't already have enough ego to keep a hang glider aloft.

This was only the second time she had met Colby in person, but she'd had enough virtual interactions with the man to know he was a pain in the ass. The smirk on his face suggested he thought he was doing Annika a favor, perhaps giving her the opportunity to further drill home her point. She didn't need his pandering. She'd rather just get back to her hotel room.

"Even considering Core profiling," Annika continued, her eyebrow cocked with barely concealed irritation, "every year the algorithms are refined, but futurists have been threatening the latest iteration will replace emotional conversation for decades."

And, every year, more and more people are losing their jobs because of it.

The worry was whether humanity was now at the tipping point of that evolution. It was highly likely they were. Vegas had been a poor city to host this conference; there was nowhere else the inevitable transition would have been more apparent.

A second notification popped up on her eye-piece.

Made a reservation. I hope that's OK. 7:30. I can't wait!!

A smile crept across Annika's face at the thought of a lovely dinner atop the structure with Cheyenne, watching the fountains below performing their elaborate display. Those moments were why she had brought her sister with her. In theory, she could have left her with Ember for the week; she was more than confident in the bot's capability. The Keeper's sole purpose was to watch out for Cheyenne. But with the events of the past few months, Annika wanted to both keep her sister close and give her the chance to experience something other than their small farming town.

Annika shook off the thought, focusing back on the

audience before her. Colby's eyes had lit up, the blue in them sparkling at her, as an all-too-enthusiastic smile beamed across his face. He leaned forward, resting his chin on the tips of his fingers, as though eager for the rest of her response.

Annika cleared her throat again and wiped the smile from her face, realizing the man had likely misinterpreted her reaction to her sister's message. She refrained from rolling her eyes.

No wonder people want to deal with bots instead of humans.

She mentally shook herself from her own thoughts and continued. "Studies continue to show that our customers prefer human interaction nine times out of ten," she replied, "regardless of the iteration of the device. When discussing their finances, people want someone they can trust, and I think we can all agree that, in lieu of recent events, trust in bots of any kind is not faring as well as it has in the past." Annika glossed over the other data points which she dared to hold only in her memory. In truth, the statistic she had shared had dipped by nearly ten points, from ninety-nine percent preferring human interaction, in only a few short years. Even with a brief increase in skepticism after the San Francisco attack, comfortability with machine intelligence had only been improving. That blip—that life-changing, destructive blip—had seemed to fade quickly into memory, and it was likely that people of Cheyenne's generation and younger wouldn't have nearly as many qualms about robotics as Annika's peers.

"But the new Core-based protocols can emulate sympathy and empathy," Colby continued. "With the bots improving with each iteration, how long will it be before they can replicate human relationships?"

Annika knew all too well the extent of the empathy bots' capabilities. Ember was example enough.

"Human interaction still has an incredibly low threat of obsolescence," Annika reaffirmed, struggling not to grit her teeth. "Humans are social beings. Our responsibility, in the current environment, is to ensure our clients receive a human touch to their banking. So, don't be afraid to implement the best practices we talked about today. Every generation has had their own challenges in adapting to new technology—we're no different. Just be willing to adapt as the world changes, and remember that even though there are things AI can do infinitely better than us, there are other characteristics that make us human; characteristics that machines can never truly replicate."

The room was quiet, and many of the faces in her eyepiece had already winked out. A few years ago, that kind of finishing statement would have earned a round of applause. Now, people were skeptical—and rightly so. The time blinked 3:30pm, and Annika was ready to call it a day.

"If they don't kill us all first!" a voice chimed in through the virtual chat.

Annika struggled to keep her face composed. *Where was the moderator?* There were far too many people on the call for the mics to be left unmuted.

Some in the crowd snickered at the remark, though others looked genuinely concerned. It was a concern for Annika, too.

The comment was beyond inappropriate. The attack on San Francisco, six weeks ago, had shaken the globe. Tens of thousands of people had been killed, and many were even claiming it was staged. Others claimed it was an inside job, possibly a way for the current administration to distract from the nation's cry for a universal basic income. As far as Annika had seen, however, the rogue bots had proven to be nothing but a ghost in the machine; a computer program gone awry. It was a problem the military had swiftly dealt with, and there had been no issues since.

But that didn't mean the wound wasn't still deep. Left unchecked, the antipathy toward AI could lead to a war of words, and this was neither the time nor the place for such matters.

Annika didn't answer the comment, but she tapped a note to the moderator on her datapad.

Did you unmute his mic?

The reply came. *Not intentionally. Sorry.*

She pursed her lips but let it go. It was best not to engage, and it seemed like a good cue to wrap things up.

"If there are no more questions, let's go enjoy Vegas. Those of you elsewhere, have a good evening."

The last of the faces winked out. The remaining attendees in the conference room didn't move. Each of them had zoned out, their attention on their eye-pieces. As though there were something happening elsewhere that had caught their attention. Or perhaps discussing the troll who had disrupted the conference channel.

Block whoever that was from the rest of the conference, Annika typed into her datapad, *and send a report to their supervisor.* The last thing she needed was for the heckling to continue in future sessions.

She packed up her datapad and turned to leave, looking up at the conference auditorium that stood between her and the exit.

Courtesy of the interruption, she had missed that Colby was still seated and had his blue eyes locked on her, staring longingly. She no longer suppressed her eye roll.

Other participants still stood about, talking, lingering before making their way to the foyer. Annika hoped their discussions were centered around the content of her presentation rather than the closing comments of some crank who had no place raising his conspiracy theories at a professional seminar.

As Annika began to mull over the best way to avoid talking to Colby, the lights in the auditorium flickered. The brief disturbance sent the man's eyes to the ceiling for long enough to give her an out. She clutched her datapad and sprinted offstage, heading for the opposite end of the dimly lit room, trying to blend in with the attendees exiting through the door furthest from his creepy gaze.

Annika looked at her datapad to avoid him. Out of the corner of her eye, she saw another tall, suited man capture Colby's attention.

Annika breathed a sigh of relief.

Despite the initial hesitancy, the seats had vacated relatively quickly, and now only a smattering of spectators remained, still browsing on their eye-pieces or through ocular implants attached to their neuro-network devices.

A brief rumbling between colleagues of something happening in New York City reached her, but she didn't think much of it. Her current aim was to avoid Colby, enjoy a relaxing drink somewhere with some of her more pleasant colleagues, and then spend the rest of the evening with Cheyenne.

Chapter 2

Annika

The doors now open, the attendees had mostly vacated the conference room and had spilled out into the foyer that separated the auditoriums. In their infinite wisdom, the conference organizer had booked a seven-thousand-capacity conference space for two thousand people. Unsurprisingly, banks had money to burn, and Annika couldn't be convinced they weren't saving on hiring fewer and fewer employees each year. The air in the hall was stale with the number of bodies crowding its space.

Annika glanced at the time on her eye-piece: 3:45pm. Anywhere else, it might have been too early to drink—but this was Vegas, after all. And they were bankers.

Annika hated reinforcing the stereotype, but sometimes they rang true. The weight of a square metal flask prodded her chest, as though reminding her it was time to let her hair down and indulge.

But there'd be no reason to use her flask again today; instead, she'd avail herself of one of the Strip's hundreds of bars. That was the major benefit of attending the conference in person, rather than dialing in virtually. It was a chance to let her hair down, insomuch she could while still looking after Cheyenne. It was a sign of her maturity that she considered two or three drinks letting her hair down these days.

"Anni!" her friend Becky called out, waving over the bodies standing between them. Becky was her sole companion from work. The brown-haired, hazel-eyed woman had been reluctant to join Annika in Sin City, but a few low-key evenings on the Strip had destroyed all doubts. "Great presentation!" she grinned, running a finger through her short curly hair. "I can't believe you stay so calm up there! What do you have, a flask of vodka hidden in that blazer?"

Annika peered around cautiously before beckoning her friend to come closer with her index finger. She couldn't help but allow a mischievous grin to cross her face.

Becky arched an eyebrow, but complied.

Annika took another quick glance around to ensure nobody was paying attention and opened her jacket a couple of inches, lifting the flask out of her inner breast pocket enough so that Becky could sport a peek at the hidden elixir.

"You're bad," Becky smirked. "Not fair! You're getting a head start!"

"Hey, I've got to be good here. I'm taking care of Cheyenne, remember?" Annika put her hands up in feigned defence. "Just a sip or two to calm my nerves. I've never presented to so many people before."

"Yeah. Virtually, you might as well have been talking to yourself."

"You'd think that'd make it easier," Annika confessed. "But the software insists on scrolling hundreds of faces through the eye-piece. It's almost *more* unnerving. Plus, you have people like Colby undressing you with their eyes."

"Great presentation, Annika." As if on cue, the compliment came from behind her.

Annika jumped as she pushed the drink back into its hiding place. She turned a shade of purple.

I hope he didn't hear that!

Colby stood behind her. A hand at the back of his neck rubbed unconsciously before moving to his jet-black hair. He was acting as if he was unsure of what to do with his hands. The sweaty paw made its way to Annika's shoulder, heat radiating from its weight. Annika did her best not to cringe, though her stomach roiled as she shrugged it off.

"Thanks, Colby," she said, biting down the urge to tear him a new one. "It was really nothing. It seems our jobs are safe until people are more willing to trust the bots."

"There are a few hundred people in the streets who I'm sure would disagree with you," he said.

Annika had almost forgotten about the protesters. The casinos' decision to do away with most human employees had put a strain on an already struggling city. "But I was talking more about your presentation skills. You always seem so calm up there. I've never been good at presenting."

Becky let out a snort, and Annika shot a dirty look at her friend. The last thing she needed was the flask in her pocket to be revealed. Though he wasn't her supervisor, Colby was technically her superior. There was no point pushing her luck.

"It comes with practice," she said. "I gave dozens of presentations at university. You just have to remember half the room isn't paying attention."

Colby let out a nervous chuckle, moving his greasy hand to fidget with a loose button on his coat jacket.

"So, I'm thinking of grabbing a drink, if you'd like to join me?" Colby said. "There's a great little bar at the Paris. It's on the way back to the Kawa. You know, under the hallway with the clouds lining the roof? I love watching the people walk through there."

Annika paused and looked to Becky, who had a dumb smirk on her face.

Was Colby seriously asking her on a date? Surely, this wasn't a work request. She didn't want to refuse, as he technically was her boss, even if not directly. But Annika had worked with enough douchebag bosses to know better than to put herself in an uncomfortable situation.

"We were just thinking of grabbing a couple of drinks ourselves," Annika replied, giving her friend a wide-eyed look.

Please. She willed Becky to hear her thoughts. *Don't leave me hanging.*

Becky grabbed her arm. "We'd really rather not talk shop," she said. "But if you have some numbers to go over, feel free to join us."

Annika breathed a sigh of relief. Becky's hand gave her shoulder a squeeze of support before returning to her side.

Hopefully, he'll take the hint and excuse himself, Annika thought. *Come if you need to talk business, but this won't be a personal exchange.*

"We hadn't picked a location," Annika said, doing her best to remain pleasant. "Where's this bar? It might be worth trying."

Colby nodded, his gaze shifting to Becky and then back to Annika, as if weighing whether the new criteria was worth the endeavor. "Yes, of course. *Le Syndicat.* Or whatever."

Damn. No such luck.

Besides the agreement of the uncomfortable meeting, Annika cringed at Colby's butchering of the French name, but she said nothing to correct him. She'd let the staff do that if necessary.

"We can split a rideshare," he said.

"How about we meet you there?" Becky asked, giving him an icy glare. "We have a few things we need to take care of first."

Colby looked a bit disappointed, and a little unsure, as though he couldn't tell they didn't want him hanging around.

"Right, well, I will see you two soon, then." He nodded awkwardly and left.

He was likely making a beeline toward *Le Syndicat,*

Annika thought, eager to have gotten a yes from her, despite Becky joining them.

Annika let out an exasperated sigh. Having a post-conference cocktail with her friend to unwind was one thing, but she resented having to spend time with a slimy sycophant who likely had other aspirations in mind besides her career path.

In reality, she'd rather have been back at the Kawa resort with her sister. She felt guilty enough for leaving Cheyenne alone for the entire day, even if it was with Ember. The android was one of a number of experimental babysitter units the Canadian government was trialing. Two hundred families in unfortunate circumstances received access to the bots. The government intended to monitor how they could be used for families in need of compassionate care.

It had made for interesting conversation as they went through Customs at the airport, but fortunately Cheyenne was brilliantly organized and had all of Ember's documentation ready.

"There's talk of lockdown," someone next to Annika had finished saying.

The snatches of conversation she'd heard on the way out of the auditorium came rushing back to her. Her heart nearly stopped.

"What's this about a lockdown?" Annika turned to the middle-aged, overweight man who had made the comment.

The man scratched the three-day stubble on his chin. It was as though he had forgotten to pack a razor and hadn't bothered to get a new one since the conference had started. The man held a beer he had somehow managed to purchase and bring back to the foyer. She didn't even think the Conference Center served liquor. Maybe he had packed it with him for this very moment.

No use in waiting to get to the bar while you're in Vegas. She contemplated whipping out her own flask, but it wasn't like she was a junior advisor. She had to set the precedent.

Annika struggled to remember the man's name until she caught a glimpse of his name tag. *Bruce*, she remembered. If her memory was correct, he hailed from Kitchener, Ontario; another fellow Canadian. Annika had noticed quite a few had opted for the in-person ticket, despite the uncertainty at the border.

Anything for a vacation, she thought.

At least her employer paid for her hotel and meals. Spooked by the San Francisco incident, many invitees had decided it wasn't worth the risk of travel and had instead cancelled and opted for the virtual ticket.

As long as he was in the conference hall, Bruce was technically on the clock, but Annika wasn't about to say anything to the man. Not with her own secret sauce pressed against her chest. The advisors were under a lot of pressure lately; she couldn't blame any of them for taking the edge off.

"You haven't heard?" Bruce asked.

"Heard what?" Annika replied. "I've been focused on the presentation. What's going on?"

"All air travel has been grounded again. The border's shut, and there's no word about when restrictions might be lifted. There are rumors more cities are preparing for lockdown." The larger man took another swig of his beer, as the grey-haired male associate he had been talking to walked away. Bruce took a step toward him, as if to follow, before Annika stopped him.

After the San Francisco incident, Annika hadn't even been sure she'd be allowed to cross the Canadian-US border until the night before her flight was scheduled. Governments worldwide had suspended all air travel, casting the conference in doubt that it might have to go completely virtual.

The attack had miraculously ended within twenty-four hours, but the damage was extensive. The onslaught had killed tens of thousands and devastated millions, many of whom had lost power and essential services. There were unconfirmed reports of similar events in China, but Beijing had clamped down their media so tight, nobody knew what to believe. After six weeks of no further incidents, mounting pressure to allow economic flow to be restored forced the hands of world leaders to ease up on the restrictions.

"*More?*" she asked. "You mean other than San Francisco?"

Despite the cessation of the drone attack, the city remained on lockdown. Understandably, the streets had been in chaos after the defective machines had wiped out a large part of the city. The President had sent the National Guard to restore order, but there were tens, if not *hundreds* of thousands, of civilians who were now without a place to live, a place to work, and with nothing to their name. FEMA was stretched to its limit trying to ensure emergency services were being provided, but the strain was unprecedented. Gangs were trying to take control of the streets. People were without power and adequate food or water. The all-encompassing destruction was devastating.

Worst-case scenarios ran through Annika's mind. If flights had been grounded, did that mean the drones were attacking again? How would she get back to Canada?

"New York, LA, Houston, among others. Nobody is saying anything about why yet, but obviously the media is speculating that the problem with the AI might not be over."

"So, what about our flights home?" Annika asked.

"The media hasn't said anything yet. They haven't even announced *why* they've been grounded. But, hey, we're not supposed to go back for a few days anyway, right? Let's enjoy our time here. I'm sure this will all be cleared up soon."

"What if they put the Strip into lockdown?" Becky asked. "Won't be much fun being here."

With her eyes wide and mouth hanging open, Becky appeared petrified. A farm girl at heart, Becky had been nervous to come to Vegas in the first place. She had never been to Sin City before, or even the United States, and everything she had seen in movies and the news had her unequivocally terrified. Despite her misgivings, Annika had somehow talked her friend into coming.

It had been especially difficult after the attack on San Francisco. Becky had been convinced they were going to die on the flight over; that some rogue government drone would shoot them out of the sky. Annika had managed to convince her those in power wouldn't open air space unless they were absolutely sure things were safe.

The trip had offered a good chance for both of them to leave town, and for Annika, it was an opportunity to hang out with an adult for once—at least during the conference. Drinks after each day of lectures had become a treat they enjoyed, and Becky had finally relaxed. In the evenings, Becky had joined Annika and Cheyenne in whatever excursions they endeavored in. The shows they went to were slightly more PG than if the two of them had been on the trip by themselves, but Becky didn't seem to mind.

"Are you kidding?" Bruce offered. "The casinos will be the last to close if they can help it. Besides, there's no point in worrying about that unless it happens," Bruce said. He took another sip of his beer. "How often do we get to be in Vegas?"

Pretty much never.

"I suppose you're right," Annika said, giving Becky a sidelong look.

"Oh, crap," Bruce cursed, his gaze suggesting something was being displayed on his eye-piece.

"What is it?" Annika asked.

"Turn your eye-piece to the news."

Both Annika and Becky complied.

At first, Annika couldn't make out much, other than a reporter on the streets of what, to her, appeared to be New York City. The ticker in the corner soon confirmed as much.

Robot attack in New York City. Three officers dead.

Annika raised an eyebrow, unsure of what she was watching. The footage showed three humanoid-looking robots shooting what appeared to be ray guns at a group of NYPD officers donned in riot gear. The scene clipped to the same bots, now deactivated, being carried off after what Annika assumed had been a shoot-out. At least it appeared the humans had won the battle.

An unprecedented attack ... the reporter was saying. *Experts are calling this an isolated incident, with no need to be alarmed. Nevertheless, New York is currently under mandatory lockdown. Houston, LA, and Miami have followed suit, though we have yet to confirm any further incidents in those cities.*

The quickening in the rise and fall of Becky's chest suggested she was careening into another panic attack.

Annika grabbed her friend's hand, and Becky jumped. Becky's brow furrowed as she looked at Annika, as though she had forgotten her friend was standing next to her.

"Becks!" she said. "It's okay. We don't even know if there's anything wrong yet. The lockdowns are probably just precautionary."

Becky nodded, but her breathing didn't slow.

"Okay, Becky, deep breath."

She complied, closing her eyes and inhaling deeply from her abdomen. Annika squeezed her hand for support.

"Let's go grab drinks with Colby." Though it was her idea, Annika couldn't suppress an eye roll. "That will be the worst thing that happens today. Then I promised Cheyenne supper at the Eiffel Tower so we can watch the fountains. We'd love it if wanted to tag along."

The promise of dinner with a view seemed to calm Becky down. She opened her eyes and looked at Annika with a smile. "That sounds nice. Are you sure we can't skip the drink with Colby, though?"

Becky winked, and then the lights in the Conference Center went out.

Chapter 3

Terre

Grand Kawa Resort & Casino — Las Vegas Strip

Terre Hoffman sat at the Sakana Tamago bar, nestled near the back of the casino of the Grand Kawa Hotel & Casino in Las Vegas, Nevada. The scotch he'd ordered was overpriced, but at least it was a single malt. High quality drink was getting harder to find as shortages of the revered beverage plagued North America.

Terre took the last sip of the golden elixir and ordered another through the datapad built into the table—it was still scotch, after all. A silver robot grabbed a bottle in its replicate hand and measured out precisely the two ounces ordered into the clean glass that emerged through a hole at the top of the counter, a ball of ice already in its center.

"Do you have anything you wish to share?" the bot asked. The metallic voice had about as much personality as Terre's shoe, and its continued feeble attempts to strike a conversation were irritating.

Terre missed the days where you could spill your troubles to a human bartender. Not that he would; his problems were his own. But at the moment, he longed for one of the few places still left where he could do so. Their locations were few, definitely not on the Strip, but even off-Strip, the choices were scarce.

Even in San Francisco, the number of human bartenders was dwindling. They could still be found, in small towns mostly, and some hipster bars still held out in Nob Hill, marketing themselves as 100% human-operated. Before the bots had blown them to bits, at least.

The machines had all but taken over what had been one of the most personable of professions. As labor costs rose and business owners became increasingly concerned with their bottom line, it was only a matter of time before restaurant owners were forced to find alternatives.

Most of the corporately owned restaurants, pubs, and bars had replaced their staff, especially the ones behind the bar. A computer could follow a mixology recipe well enough. But the same bore true for nearly every other damn job in the country. Corporate America was dead set on automating away the middle-class.

A robot bartender never complained, didn't need sick days, didn't make mistakes, and didn't need to sleep.

Behind Terre, lights continued to flash with the winnings of lucky gamblers. Cheers erupted as someone won a game of roulette, and laughter caught his ear from those who had found their own jokes to be utterly hilarious after a few drinks.

You'd almost never know that nearly the entire staff of the Grand Kawa was robotic.

Lately, Las Vegas casinos had found a newfound furor in replacing human employees. It had only been several weeks prior that the casinos had laid off every remaining employee on the gaming floor. First, one of the larger franchises on the Strip had announced the change, and the others soon followed.

Tens of thousands of workers had lost their jobs overnight, the ramifications still clear in the protesters who lined the Las Vegas Strip. Many would-be patrons had threatened to boycott the casinos over the move. Cries to support the workers over the big corporate pocketbook were sounded throughout the city, and throughout the country.

But the number of personnel gracing the casino floor told a different story.

For the visitors, it seemed almost as if nothing had changed. They still carried on, drinking and laughing. What did it matter to them who rolled the dice or served the drinks? For many, the casino floor had been a place to escape the watchful eye of people, anyhow.

But everyone from janitors to blackjack dealers were gone. The only staff Terre had seen were security guards—and most of their detail was now robotic. With the rise in unemployment and corresponding protests, even the Kawa had felt the need to increase their protective presence. Humans still felt most at ease with, and most likely to surrender to, the authority of another human.

Bots of all types had been defaced or damaged daily, from delivery bots to self-checkout machines that had all but replaced cashiers years ago. The issue had become so prominent that fines and punishments for vandalism had increased exponentially to curb the damage. It had some effect, but as more and more people lost their jobs, some felt they had little left to lose beyond their temper.

As he looked at the crude security models the hotel employed, Terre chuckled to himself. Though state-of-the-art commercial models, the bots seemed primitive compared to the prototypes he had encountered on the campus of UC Berkley weeks prior. The robotics lab of the school had been filled with lines of humanoid prototypes. Each one more haunting than the next as they ventured through the lab to upload the Guardian Program to the military's network. The end of the pilgrimage they had ventured on to put the military's out-of-control, top secret machines to rest. Those bots had been more refined, more sophisticated. The next level of autonomous beings being designed by some of the most brilliant minds on the planet.

But Terre knew that once the Sentinels had been refined and made cheap enough for the private sector, there wouldn't even be a need for human security guards. It would only be a matter of time.

Terre allowed the warmth of his scotch to sit in his mouth briefly, savoring the peated flavors and the heat of the alcohol, before letting it slide down his throat. He needed this break. He needed to get away from the horrors of Guam and San Francisco, and Vegas, though swarming with bots and protesters, was a simple choice for anyone who wanted to disappear into the crowd for a while. It didn't hurt that his new employer offered to pay for his stay and allowed him to charge alcohol to his room's tab, which was definitely something a government position would not have afforded him. There were perks to working for the private sector.

Terre was still shaken by the events in San Francisco, the second place where he had experienced a robot attack, and he hoped it would be the last.

The day after he had uploaded the Guardian program with his colleague Kristopher Klein, he'd abruptly quit his job. Terre was a code jockey, not an agent to be dispatched on death-defying missions, and he was eager to get back behind a desk.

Terre shuddered at the memory as he took another swig of whisky. He had seen more death than he ever believed was possible for a network specialist; more death than *anyone* should have to witness. But it wasn't just the mounting death toll, or the insufferable weight that had been put upon his shoulders to put a stop to it, that clawed at his insides.

The position had cost him everything.

Terre had only been a couple of months from completing his contracted term, but his boss Fredricks had reluctantly agreed to sign off on the early release without a breach of contract if he'd agreed to a psych evaluation and therapy.

Terre could hardly say no to the stipulations.

Reduced to a mere hole in the ground, San Francisco would never be the same.

Most had been struggling to get by before the attack. The fourth industrial revolution had sent the country's unemployment rate to over thirty percent in most parts of the country. It had been even higher in the Golden Gate city. For those who had survived, the attack cost them the little they had left to cling to.

Terre took another sip as he mulled over the events that had unfolded. He had tried to wipe them from his mind, tried to move forward, but it was damn near impossible to forget the image of a passenger jet hurtling into a crowded freeway or the pile of dead UC Berkeley students cut down by laser fire in the robotics lab.

That wasn't to mention his dead wife and daughter, destroyed in the previous assault on Guam. His transfer was supposed to be a momentous occasion; a homecoming for his small family. But his family was dead, and Terre had no home to speak of. His only companions were a glass of scotch and a lifeless bartender.

Terre had agreed to at least one therapy session, but it was tough finding a therapist, especially after nearly a million people had suffered the loss of their homes and neighbors being destroyed. Never mind the millions of other Americans who had watched it all unfold live through their eye-pieces and neuro implants. The human brain wasn't built to handle that level of tragedy.

The day after he had resigned, Terre received a call from an old classmate, Barry Stulman, now a senior executive at Zatica Industries, a civilian AI developer based in New York, but with offices across the country. News of his employment status had traveled fast within the industry, it seemed. Terre negotiated a few weeks of paid vacation before his start date and couldn't think of a better way to forget the last few months of his life than some downtime in Sin City. Not that it was working.

Somehow Barry got Zatica's team to agree to Terre's pre-employment vacation, on the condition that he spend several days of it at their Vegas office. They had some work he could get started on within the city itself and agreed to pay for his hotel and meals if he'd at least stop by for initial orientation, introductions, and a debrief on their top projects. It was an endeavor worth the exchange, and he was already liking the company. Being headhunted had its perks.

Terre had wanted to come to Vegas right away, though six weeks might have been a long time to spend drinking and gambling. The truth was, he had few options. Pretty much all of his possessions, aside from the few items he had with him on the Treasure Island base, had been destroyed, along with half of San Francisco. No family, no belongings, and nowhere to go. No insurance company in the country had been able to cover the extent of loss, so those who had called the city home were out of luck.

The markets had tanked, along with his investments and 401k in profits, part of the reason Zatica agreed to add him to their payroll almost immediately—they felt sorry for him. But Terre had it much better than most. A stable job, a high paying income, and, though it didn't look as good as it once had, a semblance of a retirement fund.

And even though his apartment had been lost in the siege, he had been fortunate enough to have a place to stay. Zatica would scout out a place for him to live once he settled on a final location. After the attack, he'd remained at Treasure Island temporarily. Somehow, the revived military base itself had seen only minor damage; the brunt of the impact had brought about the destruction of the Oakland bridge. There was now no way to get on or off the island other than by helicopter or by boat, so despite his resignation, his previous employers had agreed to house him short term out of respect for his conduct during the attacks on both Guam and San Fran.

An icy shiver coursed through Terre as he fought off a flashback from the early moments of the attack—a helicopter crashing on the Oakland bridge, weapons' fire sealing the road's fate, crashing it into the Bay only moments after he and his colleague, K, had crossed.

There had been so many close calls that day, it was hard to believe his luck wouldn't eventually run out. There was nothing special about him; no reason for him to have survived when so many around him hadn't made it. Nevertheless, he'd escaped the destroyed city and now sought only the solace of his own company.

Vegas had, at first, seemed like an odd choice for solitude, but Terre had visited the Strip often enough in his youth to understand that it was the perfect place to be alone, despite being surrounded by thousands of people.

So many other survivors were forced to stay in FEMA camps set up in Levi's Stadium and other sports venues. Oakland had fared little better in the attack, and with the bridges destroyed, there was no longer a convenient way to travel between the two centers.

A cheer erupted behind Terre, momentarily pulling him from his thoughts. A young couple brushed past him, clinging to each other. At first, Terre thought the glaze in their eyes was because of a newfound romance, but as he studied them closer, he realized the hollowness was darker and more disturbing than even star-crossed love could explain. Likely, the couple had made a last-ditch effort to increase their savings through gambling, an event that was becoming far too common as jobs became scarcer, and it never ended well.

Kristopher had also quit his job at NASA the day after the attack, understandably shaken from the assault. The NASA contractor had designed the AI units, originally built for space colonization, and concocted the AI reset, but afterward he hardly seemed the same. In the aftermath, he had barely spoken to Terre, simply stating he had terminated his contract and would be going off the grid for a while. K had mumbled something about disappearing into the jungles of Peru to get away from the damn bots. That was the last Terre had heard from him.

Terre couldn't say he blamed K; he sympathized with the sentiment of being as far away from tech as possible, but he wasn't about to go off grid or anything that dramatic. Terre liked the level of comfort modern life provided. Plus, he had to eat somehow; working kept food on the table. UBI was a great alternative for those who had been displaced from their rideshare and retail jobs, but it didn't provide enough of an income for someone used to the salary of a senior network specialist. But between the drone attacks on Guam and the destruction of San Francisco, Terre was ready for something more civilian. So instead of disappearing into the wilderness, he'd opted to clear his head and get back to a more normal career.

A few weeks in Vegas seemed like a great transition.

It was too bad that so much of the city's soul, whatever that meant, had been sucked out of it, replaced by the cold circuitry of bots.

The void of the robotic gray eyes behind the bar were still fixated on him, and Terre realized the bot was still waiting for an answer as to whether Terre wanted to bare his soul.

"No, thank you."

"If you need me," the bot said, "my name is Jerry. Just say 'Hey Jerry' to get my attention."

The bot took a step back, its eyes flickering before going dim, as it went into rest mode. The bot was a much cruder model than the Sentinels. Though it had a humanoid face, Jerry's countenance had been created with a rigid plastic or ceramic, not the soft synthetic flesh of the Sentinels. It was a comfort that this bot's creators weren't as concerned with trying to emulate human skin, though that was likely due to cost-reduction. Terre preferred his robots to feel more robotic than human-like. There were limits to what felt natural. The uncanny valley of robotics was real and all too apparent when cheap manufacturers tried too hard. This model seemed to have found a balance somewhere between scary and cartoonish.

Terre took another sip of scotch. It wasn't like him to bury his feelings in drink. Hell, he wished he *could* get wasted. The past few months had been particularly trying. After his wife Cara died, it had taken multiple sessions of rehabilitation, therapy, and nanobot treatments just to survive. If that hadn't been bad enough, his then employer had thrown him into a desperate attempt to save the world. He hadn't signed up for any of it. But then again, who had?

Whatever K had uploaded that night at the university had seemed to have quieted the rogue program, at least for now. There was concern the program wasn't complete, that the pause would only be temporary, but six weeks later, all was still ticking along.

Giant displays lining the top of the bar momentarily grabbed Terre's attention from his wayward thoughts. He was sure a football game had been on the display when he'd sat down, but now a newscast and talking heads had replaced it.

The news anchors were commenting on an altercation between civilians and a group of bots. Not just any bots, though—Terre would recognize those bone white frames anywhere. A handful of Sentinels lay incapacitated on the sidewalk of what appeared to be New York City.

Other casino patrons had stopped what they were doing to look at the projected screens hanging from the ceiling. Some pointed as they discussed the events unfolding onscreen, an energy of trepidation forcing its way through the crowd, reminding them that the recent troubles with AI were far from over; still a threat. The dose of reality was temporary, though. Most shrugged it off and returned to their gaming tables or whatever else they had been doing.

Though the volume on the screens was muted, the headline beneath its images read: *More rogue bots? New York City in lockdown.*

Terre cursed and downed the rest of his scotch.

Fredericks had assured Terre his and K's actions at Berkeley had provided the military with enough of a window to get the bots under control. They were supposed to have used the pause to gain access, regain control, and ensure things didn't escalate again. Who knew what that had meant, but it obviously wasn't enough.

Terre wiped his mouth and was about to pay his bill when his cell started buzzing in his pocket. Terre sighed as he reached down. He was happy for the comfort of his archaic smartphone; he had no use for the eye-pieces most of those around him sported, never mind the implants that were increasing in popularity. He already had enough tech swimming in his veins.

The Caller ID flashed, and Terre nearly dropped his phone. He held the device in his palm, weighing up whether he wanted to answer it or not. He took a deep breath before tapping the answer button on the screen.

"Fredricks," he answered. "You realize I quit, right?"

The man had been his CIA senior during his time on base in Guam, and that had continued when they were both transferred to San Francisco after the bots had destroyed the base. Fredricks had been the man responsible for sending Terre to put an end to the rogue machines. He was the last person Terre wanted to talk to, especially if Sentinels were reactivating.

"I'm guessing you've seen the news?" Fredricks asked, his husky voice straining through the receiver.

"Just now," Terre replied. "What's going on?"

"We're still trying to determine that. It seems a couple of units are coming online and not responding to us. Just like last time. Fortunately, despite what the media is saying, they haven't attacked anyone. There are rumors of downed officers, but it's unrelated. We're monitoring things until we know more."

"And let me guess, Command aren't willing to reach for the kill switch?"

"For a handful of units? That'd be overkill. A couple of Sentinels wandering around Manhattan is cause for concern, but we don't need to panic yet. So far, the drone units have shown no sign of malfunction. We'll hold off from anything drastic until we know more or until we establish there's a threat. We don't know how widespread things are yet."

Terre put his free hand to his head. "And when they do?"

"No option is off the table," Fredricks answered. "But we have to consider risk versus reward."

"Cities are on lockdown, airspace is closed … There's more happening than you're letting on."

"I don't think you realize the economic fallout if we make that call prematurely," Fredricks said, dodging the question. "This isn't like turning the lights off. It's not even like igniting a standard EMP. The NextGen3 pulses needed to knock these units out en masse produce electro-magnetic fields strong enough to ensure nothing electronic lights up for two hundred years."

Terre's frustration finally hit boiling point. "Why are you calling *me* about this, sir?"

"I know you wanted out, Hoffman, but we need your help."

Terre shook his head and rubbed his fingers over his creased forehead.

"I didn't walk off the job for a vacation, sir," he said, lowering his voice and peering around to ensure nobody was close enough to overhear him. "You hired me to run network diagnostics, not to give me ray guns and risk my ass. I left to get my head screwed on straight. Far away from these killing machines."

"You think hiding in a casino is going to keep you safe?" Fredricks barked. "You know what these things can do better than anyone."

"Yeah, which is why, whatever you're offering, I'm not interested."

"Hoffman, I've already notified Zatica. I'm waiting on some intel, but what I can tell you is going to affect you personally. Stay in Vegas and await further instructions. It's going to be all hands on deck."

"Go fuck yourself, Fredricks," Terre said, his face growing warm, though from the exchange or the alcohol, he wasn't sure. All he wanted was some time to unwind, to clear his head, then go back to a normal job and rebuild his life. Terre wasn't even sure it would be possible anymore, but he wanted to try. "Unless you've got an executive order from the President, count me out."

A sigh came from the other end of the phone. "Don't push me, Hoffman. More lockdowns may be coming. Martial law won't be off the table if more of these bots wake up again. We need you, but I haven't got clearance to divulge the specifics. Get over yourself and do your duty, son. Standby for further instructions."

The phone went silent. Terre lifted the device as if to hurl it across the casino but stopped himself mid-swing. Getting kicked out wouldn't help him, as tempting as destroying his phone might be.

"Work troubles?" a woman's voice chimed from behind him.

Artificial Insurgence
Order your copy today

ACKNOWLEDGMENTS

The Guardian Program is a short read, but a lot of work went into bringing it to the final stage of production. Although The Guardian Program is the fourth book I've published, it was the second I'd written.

Since its original drafting it's gone through multiple revisions, expansions and deletions to bring it to the work that you've read today.

I'd like to thank Pete Smith from Novel Approach Manuscript Services for providing it with multiple edits, and assisting with details and phrasings that I was at a loss for. His efforts have truly brought this work to the next level of refinement.

To Aime Sound at Red Leaf Word Services for the final proofread and catching my Canadian-isms before the book hit the shelves.

The folks at MiblArt have been my cover designers from the beginning, and they outdid themselves with the covers for this series.

And as always to my lovely wife Nettie, who understands

my early mornings, late evenings, and weekends at the keyboard. It is truly a blessing to have someone so supportive behind me.